Storyland Shorts Collection

Storyland Shorts Collection

Indigo Dylis

And

Erika Wilson

Indigo Dyis
2014

Copyright © 2014 by Indigo Dylis

All rights reserved. This book or any portion thereof may not be reproduced or used in any manner whatsoever without the express written permission of the publisher except for the use of brief quotations in a book review or scholarly journal.

First Printing: 2014

ISBN: 978-1-326-10275-3

www.narrativecity.com

1
THE FIRST PAGE
BY INDIGO DYLIS

Every story has to start at page one. Every melody has a first note. Even the greatest heroes, like the mighty Maximus Damage, or the awesome Captain Stormcrow, had simple, private lives before the whirlwind took them and showed them the stars. Many of us dream, but no-one ever expects to end up as a famous hero, not really. And, of course, by the time we do we're too busy trying the live through it to worry about the fame and the loot.

I saw Stormcrow once. I was playing for small change on a street somewhere in the Far East, hoping to be noticed by some lantern-jawed noble with deep pockets and a thing about red-haired musicians, though I'd have settled for enough cash for a bath and a few nights in a real bed.

He strode past me, as if he'd stepped out of a story from my childhood, his swash buckled like nothing I'd ever seen and the cares of the world written in his deep, dark eyes. For months afterwards, I was afflicted with horribly exquisite dreams of moonlight and music through still summer nights on the deck of the Broken Heart. As it happened he was out of sight before I'd shaken the brownies out of my guitar, and he never got to hear any of the songs I wrote for him. We move in similar circles now, so maybe I will play them for him some day.

 By the time I found my own first page, there was half a decade and a thousand miles between me and that star-struck kid. I was a seasoned traveler by then, wise, strong and capable or at least that was what I thought. I followed my feet to Narrative City, the bright, burning hub around which everything in Storyland Revolves.

On arrival in a new city I like to spend at least a day exploring, getting a feel for the place, but in NC it isn't possible to scratch the surface in that sort of time. I tried; I shared a liquid breakfast, a lot of laughter and a game of lingerie poker with the ladies of the Gravestone Saloon. I sat outside the Starbucks in Central's Rosemary Square and watched the crazy people shouting at each other while I ate my chocolate muffin. I took a sky taxi over the Neon Gate and the driver bent my ear in a barely comprehensible stream while casually dodging oncoming traffic and nipping between the towering glass and steel hyperscrapers. I jammed with a vampire rock band in an all-night café near Jekyll's Gate. I strolled by moonlight down Lover's Lane, and it almost broke my heart when I kissed the inevitable handsome stranger goodbye.

Eventually, though, as most eastern visitors to NC tend to do, I made my tired way back to the more familiar wonders and dangers of Eastside, and the warm, welcoming embrace of the Green Dragon Inn.

The Dragon was one of only three buildings in Eastside to have more than three storeys, and its hulking timber frame dominated the market square. The main bar took up most of the ground floor. It was a vast space, filled with weathered wooden tables with a long bar at one end and a low stage at the other. I arrived sometime in the small hours, when the last of the evening's revelers had retired and preparations for another hectic day were just beginning. I placed my guitar on the polished oak bar and waited patiently for the landlord to finish stacking wine bottles. At length he stood up and turned around. He took a long slow look at my unkempt hair and travel stained clothes, stopping by the selection of daggers in my belt and the short sword at my hip. His teeth glinted in the candle light as he smiled. When his gaze came to rest on my guitar case he said, in a brisk, business like tone,

"Three nights a week, background music winding up to a full performance late in the evening, and you play until the punters have had enough, not until you run out of songs. You get free room and board, and you can stay for as long as people wanna hear you play. Deal?"

"How did you know?" I asked through my tired grin.

"Oh I knew you'd be along sometime, miss. Our last bard, Frankie, skipped town three days ago, muttering something about doing it his way. This kind of thing happens a lot around here. I'm Joe, welcome to the Green Dragon," he said, wiping his hands on his apron and holding one out to me.

"I'm Alice," I said, returning his firm handshake.

"Well, Alice, you look about ready to drop. Take any room on the top floor, they're all empty at the moment."

I left him with a grateful nod, lifted my bag and my guitar and made my way up the stairs.

Later that day I woke, washed, and was dragged down the stairs by the smell of a hearty breakfast. The Dragon had provided the blueprint for taverns all over the east of Storyland, and it was therefore no surprise to find that their cooking was designed to fortify the weary in preparation for a hard day's hacking and slashing. I found an enormous pile of spiced potatoes, scrambled eggs, smoked fish and bacon waiting for me when I reached the main bar. I washed it all down with several mugs of rich, dark ale while I took the measure of the customers currently in the bar.

There weren't many of them, it still being fairly early in the morning. A group of dwarves had staked out a corner near the stage, and were already slinging back the hard stuff, getting bits of greasy meat stuck in their beards and occasionally chanting and banging on the table.

An old man in a badly fitting but expensive green suit was clearly here for business reasons, and something in his manner suggested that he was here every day. I wondered briefly what he was buying and selling, and if I needed to worry about his presence.

The young oak of a man standing alone at the bar was another prospect altogether. He looked around constantly, peering out from behind a curtain of long black hair, and he twisted every few minutes so he could look at the door. His hand was never too far from the enormous sword he had propped up against the bar. As the serving girl topped up his ale he favoured her with a warm, gentle smile. The gesture was strangely at odds with the armour and the weaponry, not to mention the nervousness. I was sufficiently intrigued to approach him, and as I did I felt a strange sensation in my stomach and my fingers. Something was happening here, I could feel it. Something important.

"Waiting for someone?"

He looked startled when I spoke, but he didn't reflexively reach for his sword as I had expected. Instead he brushed the long, silky mane away from his face and smiled nervously.

"I ... I think so," he said with almost childish uncertainty.

"You think so?" I said, raising an eyebrow and putting just a touch of laughter in my voice. I moved a bar stool closer to him and set my ale down on the bar.

"I know it sounds dumb, I just ... I have this feeling that I'm supposed to be here today, y'know?"

"Do you often have these 'feelings'?" I said, keeping my voice light even as my stomach did back-flips.

"Never before. I was actually thinking of heading home."

"Really?"

"Yeah. It's just so hard working out who the good guys are. I never know who I should be helping and who needs a slap. I'm tired of getting it wrong and I'm starting to think that life as a blacksmith wouldn't be so bad. But I passed by this place and I had this feeling ... sorry, you must think I'm nuts. It just feels ... right... to be talking to you about this."

"Not at all," I said, lifting my drink to hide my worried expression, "I spend most of my life following feelings like that and I often thought it would have been easier if I'd stayed at home and married dad's apprentice like I was supposed to. But y'know, there just has to be more to life than making barrels. I'm sure when you look back it'll all make sense. You just have to trust yourself..." I trailed off when I realised I was babbling too. Why was it so important to me that this kid didn't go home? Why was the back of my brain insisting that I should protect him? I mean, had it seen those muscles?

"Thanks," he said, beaming. "I'm Martin."

"Really? You look more like a 'Grod' to me," I said lifting my cup again and clinking it on his. "Nice to meet you, I'm Alice."

"So what brings you here, so early in the morning?"

"I'm scoping out my audience. I'm playing here this evening."

"Maybe I'll stick around after all." He said, colouring a little as he played his words back in his head. "I … erm… I meant for the music."

"Relax Grod," I said with a playful pat on his hand, "I know what you meant." And with that I slid off the stool and went to fetch my guitar.

I spent the rest of the morning, and most of the afternoon on the roof outside my window, tuning up and thinking about what I would play. This wasn't strictly necessary, since by then my repertoire was large enough that I could play all night if I had to, and any real tavern musician chooses individual songs on the fly, depending on the mood and culture of the audience. What I was really doing was keeping my fingers busy and my internal monologue silent while I tried to work out what had happened with young Martin and how I felt about it.

It was an interesting vantage point, overlooking the market square, where the street-life of Eastside happened. There were a dozen different languages drifting up to me from the market place, and the variety of peoples and dress was enough to make my head spin, well travelled as I was. As I finished tuning and began idly picking the strings, I watched a fruit seller arguing with a priest over a display of watermelons, and a group of street kids systematically picking pockets and disappearing into the crowd. I should have come here years ago. This was my kind of town.

And then again, something was going to happen tonight and I didn't know what it was. I had learned to trust feelings like this, and I knew it could mean a chance to fulfill my dreams or it could leave me in a world of pain. I had to know what I could expect, or at least if I should run for the hills. I felt a tingle of excitement run through my fingers as I reached for my power. I felt the magic form around me as the music become more complex, and when I was ready I asked my question.

Should I stay or should I go?

When I'd composed myself and wiped the grin off my face I made my way down the stairs again, past the now hectic bustle of the residential floors and ignoring the intriguing hush from behind the heavy door of the private bar.

I nodded to Joe on my way into the main bar room. He was holding court at the end of the bar while his staff took care of his customers. I took a moment to look around. It was still early in the evening, and the room was still reasonably quiet, though it would take an awful lot of people to make this room feel crowded.

The rattle and clack of a vigorous dice game dominated the room. People crowded around the table, side-wagers fluttering around the periphery like wind stirring a wheat field. Watching the action with obvious interest, Martin stood out from the crowd, simply because, as small as he might try to make himself, he was a crowd. A pack of well-dressed young pups clustered on his lee side, testing him with veiled insults that bit steadily deeper as Martin's stoic forbearance emboldened them. I felt the heat rise into my own face on his behalf and wondered what sort of warrior he was to allow it. I think back on that moment with shame. I had a lot to learn -- about what makes a warrior and why Martin was destined to belong among the best of them. It wasn't time for the main show yet so, as per Joe's brief, I chose a seat close to the game table and began picking my guitar, beginning with a gentle, unobtrusive phrase, repeated over and over.

The game was about to erupt, mostly because one of the players was cheating with obvious glee, and not bothering to be subtle about it. The culprit was currently allowing a smug smile to play on his handsome face. He was dressed in black velvet and was wearing altogether too much jewelry, much of it magical if my music could be believed.

"You cheated, those dice are loaded," growled the dwarf to his right. This dwarf was very different from the revelers I noticed earlier. They were still here in fact, making a lot of noise from their corner by the stage. This one was sober and he wore the horned helm and forked beard of a dwarven war priest. At this realisation, something began to niggle at the back of my mind. This was a new piece of the puzzle, but I didn't know where it fitted yet.

I still haven't found what I'm looking for. I felt that magical tingle ran through my fingers again.

The young man looked over at me briefly, a puzzled look on his face. Then he turned back to the dwarf. "Loaded?" he said, as if insulted, "why would I bother with a cheap trick like that?"

He raised a finger and the dice flipped over, changing Orc-eyes to Elf-toes. "An easy thing to do." In the same manner, the money in the pot redispersed itself. "Gentlemen," he said, holding up his own well-filled purse. "I believe this game may have run its course, drinks all around?" The loud, appreciative laughter of the dwarf who'd accused him of cheating discouraged the incipient grumbling from the crowd. And no one really wanted to be on the wrong end of an argument with both a war priest and a mage, especially when there was free beer to be had.

The sense of potential violence had subsided, but I was still humming like a plucked string. Something was happening, something important. A war priest and a mage. A war priest and a mage and a warrior.... and a bard. The copper piece dropped, and I realised what was happening.

Barely daring to breathe, I watched the dwarf, waiting to see what he would do next. He downed his pint, wrung the excess out of his beard and slapped the mage heartily on the back.

"What's your name boy?"

The mage, still coughing at the force of the blow, said

"Jon. Jon O'Than. And you, erm … father?"

"I have no title, boy, not out here. My name is Kordon Badaxe. That was a nice trick, so why reveal it?" Neither man noticed that the noise from the other dwarves had abruptly stopped.

"It's no fun being clever if nobody knows about it, and I was never going to actually steal your money – that would be wrong," said Jon with mock sincerity.

"You know, I think I like you kid..."

At the dwarf table, the audible pocket of silence had become a flurry of consternation, then a series of chairs scraping back, several tipping over backwards. Kordon pulled the mage away from the table just as a throwing axe embedded itself into the thick wood, a fountain of splinters, glass and dice spouting upwards. The room erupted as everyone scrambled for cover or reached for their own weapons.

"Badaxe!" The other dwarf's voice was slurred with drink, but his feet were planted firmly and the grip on his second throwing axe looked dangerously steady. "You shouldn't be here, priest. You were ordered to leave the city!"

Sensing a private dispute, the crowd parted, leaving Jon, Kordon and Martin facing a phalanx of drunk, heavily-armed dwarves.

"No," said Kordon calmly, pulling the hammer from his belt and placing it deliberately on the table. "I was ordered to leave the Undercity," He stepped towards the speaker, empty hands held out wide. "Your king has no authority here. He is weak and fearful and allows himself to be dominated by small-minded cretins like you, but I will not. I face you with open hands, and I do not fear you. Can you say the same?"

"You sided with the humans against the dwarves!"

"I sided with a defenceless child against three armed thugs."

"He was a thief!"

"He was a starving little boy. Stand down."

"Pah! We'll kill you!"

"Drop your weapons, or you will die today."

Jon was chanting under his breath, and Martin was moving smoothly towards the hearth, opening his line of sight on the group of drunken dwarves. I realised that the music I was playing had changed, from a simple background pattern to the more complex notes I used in my magic. This was a calming melody, and I could see it working. They were coming back from the brink, but the retreat was slow and violence could still erupt at any moment. I couldn't fail to notice that we were working together already, seamlessly and without a word spoken, but there was someone missing. We weren't ready yet. And then I noticed, high in the rafters and hidden among the smoke and shadows, the glint of firelight on an arrowhead, and the gleam of large, almond shaped eyes. The last of us had arrived after all.

Here we are now, said the magic in my music, *entertain us.*

A black fletched arrow thudded into the floorboards just inches from the lead dwarf's boot.

"It's four against seven, and I can drop two of you before you can close to strike. You face magic, and the power of your own gods as well. Put your weapons down!" said a commanding, feminine voice from above our heads. It was a nice try, but our stealthy friend clearly didn't know a thing about dwarves. They charged.

In the end, it didn't last long. Two of them fell to arrows before they got close to Kordon, and another two were went down as black lightening shot from Jon's outstretched hand with a deafening clap of thunder. Martin intercepted the other three with an expertly hurled table while I was still carefully setting my guitar aside and Kordon stood, braced to receive the charge, hands glowing red with divine power.

The archer dropped from the rafters, crouched to absorb the impact, and stood in one graceful movement. She was clearly elven, and very striking, with piercing green eyes, dark hair and pale skin, which gave off a subtle blue glow. She still held her bow in her right hand and her barely decent leather "armour" bristled with an arsenal of gently curved blades.

"I am Alea Twilight, Princess of the Deep Forest." She announced.

Wordlessly, Kordon moved the table aside and began to examine the fallen dwarves. He clasped his hands together, murmuring sonorously. Power crackled between his palms as he called upon the healing power of his god. These dwarves would have killed him without mercy, and he expected no thanks for this difficult task, but he would save them if he could.

"Do they really deserve your help?" asked Alea. She, like the rest of us, had a great deal to learn.

"It isn't their fault. They were drunk, and they're badly led," said Kordon bitterly.

"You were wrong, by the way," said Jon, "when you said there were four of us. Actually, we are five." He turned to me and winked, the smug smile once again flitting across his young face.

I found Joe crouched behind the bar, though it seemed this was merely a sensible precaution, since when he saw me and stood up he appeared just as unruffled as ever.

"Joe, I think me and these people have a lot to talk about. Could we use the private bar?"

He scratched his head while he surveyed the damage, and the space where his customers used to be.

"I'm going to be waiting for another bard to turn up aren't I?"

Maybe tomorrow, I'll wanna settle down...

"It's possible," I said.

"Of course you can. The door is enchanted, but we had a problem a few weeks back and the password is carved on the top of the doorframe. Don't tell no-one."

At length, the five of us gathered in the private bar, which was a small, intimate space on the first floor with a few tables and a cabinet sporting a selection of bottles and an honesty box. Out of habit, I chose a seat in the corner and began picking a tune. As Martin ducked under the door frame I shot him a smile,

"Nice moves down there, Grod." My smile widened as he reddened and smiled back.

"I'd appreciate it if we didn't have any music right now," said Jon, opening a bottle of wine, setting some more on the table and leaving enough gold to buy a small vineyard in the box. "At least until I know the limits of what you can do with it. Sure you understand."

"Of course, sorry," I said, resting my fingers on the strings. Kordon was the last to arrive, looking pale and exhausted behind his huge blond beard. I wasn't surprised after his battle to save our fallen attackers.

"So what's happening?" Asked Alea, "One little scrap and we're suddenly bestest buddies? Isn't that a little…"

"No, it's a lot," I said, "And that's how we know it's really happening, "Look at us, every role is filled." I pointed at myself. "Rogue."

Then Martin. "Warrior."

Jon. "Mage."

Kordon. "Cleric."

Alea. "Ranger."

I paused, letting the moment sink in. I plucked a single note and let it hang in the air,

Come together - right now.

"I really can feel something," said Martin. It's like I was meant to meet you people. And down there, we all just stepped up to protect each other. It was… well it just felt right."

"I have to agree with Grod," said Jon. Martin didn't correct him and he went on, "Something definitely happened downstairs, to all of us. Princess, why did you intervene in an argument between dwarves? Grod, why did you step in to help? Kordon, how did you know we'd back you up? I know some things about magic, and enchantment doesn't feel like this. This is something bigger, something older. "

"I felt it too. I can still feel it," said Kordon, looking around fiercely. "This is the start of a story. Isn't this why we all came here tonight? To get involved in something?"

All eyes turned to Alea, the single dissenting voice. She sat down and took a goblet of wine from the table.

"Ok, I'm with you. Two questions, though," she said, green eyes lighting up with mischief, "What shall we do next, and more importantly, what shall we call ourselves?"

I could tell it was going to be a long night. With a contented sigh I picked a few more notes.

It's all right now, my magic rang the truth I felt, *baby it's all right now.*

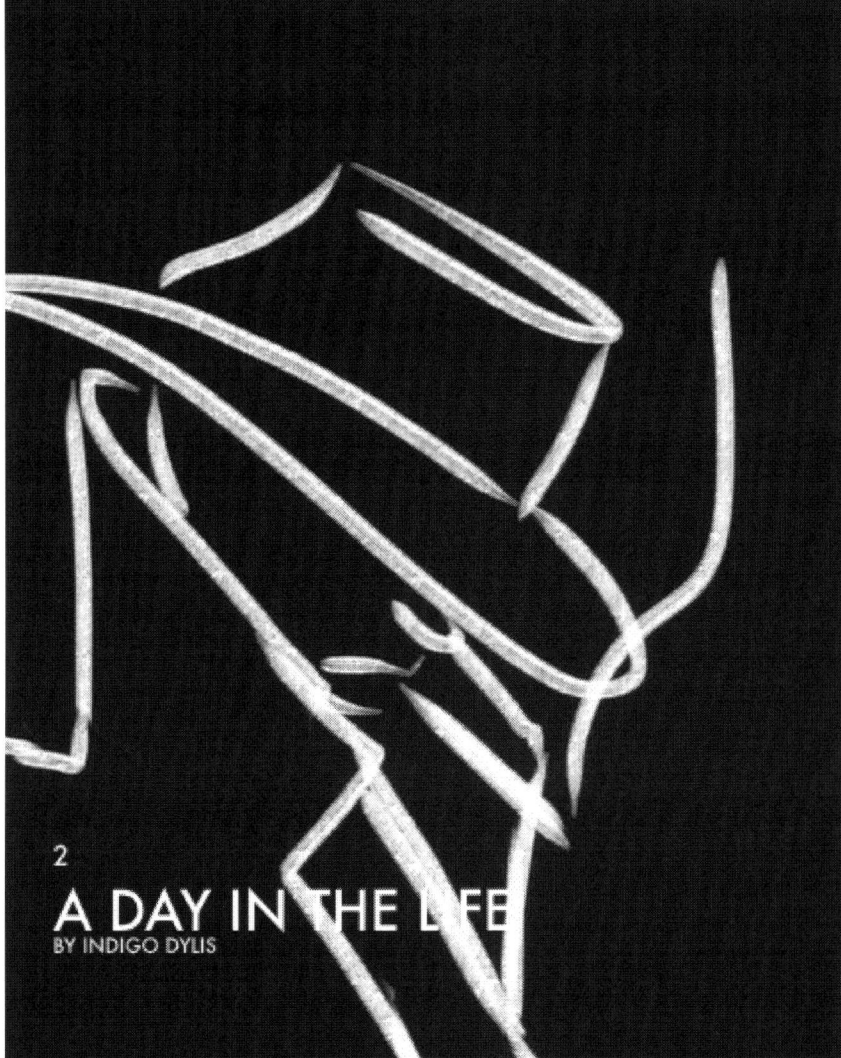

Detective Jack Nightfall looked around the dingy room, frowning through his headache and fighting the urge to reach for the pills in his jacket. He needed a drink, preferably one that came in several different bottles. As his eyes drifted around the circle of uncomfortable chairs it was like looking into thirteen slightly twisted mirrors. The room was full of well worn denim and leather, with more overt cynicism and concealed weaponry than a Gristle Street brothel. With one notable exception, every face sported at least two day's worth of stubble and the scents of cheap whisky and cigarette smoke mingled to create a unique nasal experience that could only be found here, in this room, every other Tuesday night.

According to the ancient and arcane traditions of such gatherings, he was supposed to stand up and introduce himself. It seemed foolish somehow, since everyone here was capable of working out the broad strokes for themselves. There were not many circumstances that could have led him here, and little details were what these people did.

The notable exception raised a perfectly shaped eyebrow in Jack's direction and he felt his mouth lift at the corners. Viewed in the right light, that gesture held the ghost of a promise about the future. But Narrative City held a special place in her heart for people like them, and a very specific destiny awaited those who survived long enough to end up in this room. That destiny didn't look hopeful. These people didn't waste their time chasing happy endings. Shaking his head and reaching for uncharacteristic sincerity, Nightfall stood up and said the all important words.

"Hi, I'm Jack, and I'm a detective."

"Hi Jack," thirteen voices mumbled.

"I lost my partner last year, and I've been finding it difficult to move on," he said to nods and muttered support. "I can't let it go. I can't let anything go. I have no relationships to speak of. I have colleagues and contacts where other people have friends. I have nothing but my pride to keep me warm at night and nothing but the bottom of a whisky glass to go home to. And if I survive the street for long enough, I won't even have the job any more. I'll be sent on my way with a handful of stories and a gold watch, and I'll spend my last few years going slowly senile while I hope and pray for one last case, so I can feel alive and useful again."

"So why do you do it?" asked the notable exception. Her voice was clear and assured, more gentle than he'd expected, but it held the complex note that said she knew the answer and she just needed to hear him say it.

"Because it's what I am. Because I don't know how to do anything else. And because somebody has to," he said. He lifted his eyes to hers and he felt the last tattered vestiges of his defiance gather in response to her sad, approving smile. "I'm Jack. And I'm a detective," he said softly as he sat down.

The meeting continued for another hour, and when the other detectives had talked out their troubles they adjourned to the Blue Oyster, where policemen had been self-medicating for generations. Jack considered joining them, but instead he accompanied the lady to a smaller, more intimate bar.

He knew her name by now, or at least he knew the name she'd given him. There were other details that weren't real as well. Beautiful as those vivid green eyes were, he was pretty sure she was wearing contacts, the rich chocolate colour or her hair almost certainly came out of a bottle, and her Eastside accent was very nearly perfect. It was an accomplished disguise, but not good enough to fool him. He had no doubt that the effect was quite deliberate.

"So, Matilda. What brought you to the burnout room?" he asked as she lined up the shots again and lifted one to her lips.

"What makes you think I didn't tear my life down like the rest of you?" she replied, cocking her eyebrow again as another brimming glass of the hard stuff disappeared.

"Fair enough. So what brings you to a room full of detectives, wearing an incomplete disguise with a subtly inconsistent backstory?"

"Sheesh, Nightfall, a girl dyes her hair and tells a few harmless lies and suddenly you're all suspicious? I'm starting to see why people say policemen are tiresome."

"You do know what that meeting was, right?"

"Yes I get it, Jack. You're the great Jack Nightfall and you're not fooled. Well done. Since you ask, I was looking for someone like you. A DA meeting seemed like the perfect place to start."

"Like me? Let me guess," he said, helping himself to a shot and grimacing as it burned a trail down his throat. "You love the smell of failure in the morning."

"Oh honey," she said, taking hold of his shirt and pulling him down to kiss her, "You don't know how to fail, any fool can see that. And in any case, I'll be long gone by the morning." He would realise later that he'd quite forgotten to ask her who she really was.

Jack awoke to find his flat predictably devoid of mysterious women. True to her word she was indeed long gone, leaving behind a faint scent of jasmine, some minor bruises and abrasions and a small brown envelope containing the key to a long term locker at the spaceport. Jack's curiosity was running dangerously high, particularly given what he could remember of last night, but he had no intention of blindly rushing into someone else's adventure. Instead he took a wine glass from the coffee table and a long, dark hair he found in his bed, carefully sealed them in evidence bags and made the short drive into Central Station.

He was pleasantly surprised as he slid his mustang into place. He'd expected someone to have stolen his spot, parking places being an important indicator of relative status among the many competing DIs working out of Central and this one being in prime position, just a few strides away from the lift. He took the lift up to the lab and interrupted the infuriatingly glamorous Dr. Jane Smith. She looked up from her microscope, brushed a wisp of red hair away from her delicately freckled nose and frowned at him.

"Jack, you're not supposed to be here."

"How do you know?"

"Because everyone tells me everything. If Foley had signed your sheet I'd know it."

"Look, I just need a small favour."

Her frown deepened.

"Just a finger print and a DNA test," he said, "And I need them both running against the mainframe."

"Is that all?" she deadpanned. "Any more resources you want me to misuse? What's it for?"

"Someone wants me to get involved in something, and I want to find out more about them."

"With a DNA test? Can't you just stalk her on Facebook Like a normal person?"

"Other social networking sites are available," he said sternly.

"Indeed," agreed Dr. Smith with a shrug of her shoulders.

"Look," he said, holding up the bag with the wine glass in it. "The fingerprints on this will tell me who she wants me to think she is," he paused to hold up the bag with the hair sample in it, "and this will tell me who she really is."

"Assuming she has a record."

"I'd bet my Phantoms tickets on that," said Jack, flashing his famous winning smile. Smith took the bags from Jack and handed them to one of many nondescript minions.

"You won't want to be hanging around too long I expect. Give us two hours to turn it around, and stay the hell away from Foley. He'll skin you alive if he finds out you're working a case."

"Thanks, Jane. I owe you one."

"Do me a favour, Nightfall, and resist the urge to do me any favours," said Smith, smiling almost against her will, "I don't need your kind of trouble."

Jack waited outside the lab, mostly because moving around the station would inevitably bring his presence to the attention of his volatile commander, and he was under orders to stay away until he'd been passed as fit for duty. This followed a disastrous indecent in the canteen and the psyche evaluation it prompted. Everyone was very sorry, of course. They were sorry that Danny Sundown had been eaten by a vampire. They were sorry that said vampire was Jack's former lover, which meant he had effectively lost the two most important people in his life. But the challenges of policing a multi-genre society meant that sometimes things like this would happen, and those challenges needed safer hands than those of a DI who exploded at the mention of garlic in the soup.

So Jack was expected to stay away, go to his meetings and wait for the NCPD to decide that the city needed him again. But what if that never happened? What if this was the end?

Such thoughts raced around his mind for some time, as he paced up and down the corridor, tracing a repeated path between the vending machines. Eventually Dr. Smith came and found him.

"Jack," she said, her face full of sympathy.

"What happened?" he asked, wondering what he could possibly have left to lose that could make her look like that.

"Foley is waiting for you."

"What?"

"The fingerprint and the hair. They come from the same woman. She's dead, Jack. She jumped from the Hyde Bridge in the early hours of this morning. I'm so sorry."

"No, in the early hours of this morning she was carving my back up with her fake nails," he said. "The woman I met didn't kill herself. She wasn't the type."

Dr. Smith shrugged. "All I know is that the samples you brought in match the body we have downstairs, and you have to go talk to Commander Foley. Now, Jack."

"Who was she?"

"We believe she's a waitress called Matilda Bennett but it isn't official yet. Next of kin are expected any time."

"Who's coming?"

"Jack, I ..."

"Please, Jane. She ... or someone ... brought this to my door. I have to do my best for her and that means I need to know it all. Everyone tells you everything. Who's coming?"

Smith nodded slowly. "Ok, Jack. For Matilda, not for your ego, I'm going to help you but not here. Pick me up at eight and I'll give you everything I can. Now go see Foley before he loses it."

"I'm going. Thanks, Jane."

"Go!"

Ordinarily, Jack would have wanted to examine the body before facing the commander, just so he knew for certain if she was last night's playmate. However something in Dr. Smith's tone got through to him and he decided not to push his luck. Foley could be a real monster sometimes.

He was relieved to find the main office relatively calm, considering it was the hub of the largest police force in Storyland. It seemed the old man was holding it together, again relatively speaking.

As Jack approached his desk, Foley opened the glass door to his office and bellowed,

"Nightfall! Get in here!"

Jack slid though the door and took his customary place, standing by the window in stoic silence while he waited for the storm to blow out. It didn't take that long, as it happened and in a few minutes Foley stopped shouting and Jack was able to hear again through the ringing in his ears.

"I'm just worried about you, Jack," said Foley in a more subdued voice, lowering his massive bulk into his chair and resting his elbows on his desk. It was another new one, Jack noticed. "I'm worried about your judgement, about what you might do. I know I can't stop you getting involved in this thing, but it's my duty to try. Leave your gun and your badge, and go home, Jack."

"Sir, I know I'm not in the best place right now but that's because you won't let me do my job. I've tried to do what you asked, spend my time smoking cigarettes and watching Captain Kangaroo but it didn't work. This case found me anyway."

"That's why I advised you to leave the city for a few weeks, but you didn't listen, did you? Your gun and your badge, Jack.

Keep your head down, show me you can follow orders even when you don't like them, and then we'll talk about getting you back out there, ok?"

"Sir, there's something going on. The woman I met last night must have planted..."

"See Constable Firble before you go and provide him with a statement. We'll fit your ... encounter into our ongoing investigation."

"But ..."

"We'll be in touch if we need anything further ... Mr. Nightfall."

Mr. Nightfall. He couldn't be Mr. Nightfall. Mr. Nightfall was an overweight security guard pretending he was still a cop, eating doughnuts all day while the shoplifters outwitted him and the store manager docked it from his wages. Mr. Nightfall was what happened when Detective Jack Nightfall couldn't cut it anymore, when he couldn't find his way back, when he could no longer see past what he'd been through and remember why he went through it. Mr. Nightfall was a loser's name. Jack, whatever he might be, was no loser. Jack Nightfall always won, that's how he knew the story was finished.

He placed his badge and revolver on Foley's new desk.

"How many times is that now, sir?" he said with a defiant grin.

The Commander sat back in his chair and chuckled, genuinely amused. "Got to be five at least. You never learn, and you always prove me wrong."

"I always had Danny with me before."

"Of course. Nightfall and Sundown. My best guys. Of course I couldn't tell you. You were a pair of egomaniacs as it was."

Jack hesitated, uncomfortable with this sudden vulnerability, and yet somehow unable to hold it back. "I miss him, sir."

"I know, kid. So do I. But he's gone, and he's not coming back, and I don't want you to join him."

"I'll see you on the other side, sir."

"I'm choosing to believe that you're going home, as I damn well instructed you to. Be careful, Jack."
"And you, sir," said Jack as he closed the door.

Jack made a short stop at his flat, to pick up a replacement sidearm and Danny's badge, which he had kept in a strongbox in his spare room since Danny's little sister had asked him to look after it. He felt like a heel as he slid it into his jacket, but there was nothing for it - where he was going he would need a badge. Danny would get it. He'd probably have done the same thing.

The area of Narrative City known as "The Spaceport" was actually more like a small, indoor town with a giant elevator connecting an orbital docking station to the adventure and shopping opportunities available in Storyland's greatest city. It was effectively isolated from the rest of the city, in a way that the other provinces didn't even attempt. While inter-stella travellers were allowed, on their promise to obey certain rules, to enjoy the wonders of NC, the natives were most certainly not allowed to peer behind the curtain. The first rule of Space Club? Don't talk about Space Club. Jack only knew anything more than rumours because occasionally spacemen committed crimes, just like everyone else.

He hit the tunnel leading to the main gate doing fifty, acutely aware that half a dozen cameras were tracking his mustang as he approached. When he reached the gate he flashed Danny's badge at the security droid, and because he didn't know how sophisticated it was he said,

"Detective Daniel Sundown, NCPD."

The droid beeped and spluttered for a few moments and then the gate slid smoothly aside.

He was met in the long-stay car park by a strapping six-footer in skin-tight blue and white lycra, a complex looking utility belt at his waist.

"Let me guess," said Jack as he slammed his car door, "blonde hair, smile straight out of a 1950's toothpaste commercial, a jawbone you could bounce a bowling ball off, smug self satisfaction oozing from every pore… you're a fighter pilot, right?"

"Actually I'm a starship captain, but I used to fly fighters," said the spaceman "Y'know, before I went all respectable. Ok, my turn," he said, making a pantomime of looking Jack up and down, "boxer's build, but you drink heavily and eat a lot of rubbish. A few subtle scars, slug thrower almost concealed in your worn leather jacket, several days of stubble, you have a detective's badge and bad attitude - so you're a burned out cop, right? Actually from the look of you I'm surprised you still have your badge."

"Ok, close enough. I think you won that one, captain?" said Jack, offering his hand. The spaceman shook it enthusiastically.

"Alex Rodgerson, of the starship Mona Lisa. My friends call me Rod."

"Nice to meet you, Captain Rodgerson," said Jack, taking his hand back with some difficulty. "I'm Detective Danny Sundown."

"No, you're not."

"Pardon?"

"You're Jack Nightfall. The two of you helped one of my guys out a few years ago - case of mistaken identity whilst being naughtily drunk. I was very sorry to hear about your partner. As I recall he didn't like me very much but he was a good man. Now, could be I can guess why you're flashing Detective Sundown's badge about, but I'm not going to try. Starship crews go through a lot together, and you saved one of mine. I owe you a favour - that's why I came down here when I heard who was at the door. Now, detective, what do you need?"

Jack took the key from his jacket. "I'd like to find the locker that goes with this key."

"May I?" said Rod, holding out his hand. Jack handed him the key. "Level ninety seven. That's above the line."

"The line?"

"Sorry. Nobody gets above level eighty without flight clearance. Whoever rented this locker was either a crew member on a starship, or station staff. I'm afraid your borrowed badge won't get you up there, but I'll go clear it out and bring it's contents to you. Come on, I'll show you a nice quiet bar you can wait in."

A few hours later Jack was back in Dr. Smith's lab, getting her most severe death-stare.

"I can't believe you came back here, you insufferable little cretin. You obviously have no concern for your own career, but what about mine? I said I'd meet you…"

"No time, Jane. Has Miss Bennett's identity been confirmed yet?"

"Yes, her employer came in just after you left."

"Her employer?"

"Yes. No family, no friends. No records at all until recently but you know what this city is like. She worked at the Moonlit Cafe in Valentine Square."

"Of course she did. Lover's Lane is where all the desperate lonely people go."

"Where are you going with this?"

"If I'm right her real name was Georgia DeBrett. She was a shuttle pilot working out of the Spaceport. Three months ago her brother flew in from a galaxy far, far away and was killed in what looked like a random bar fight. She disappeared the same day, but apparently nobody thought to look for her at the Moonlit Cafe. Then last night someone pretending to be her secret identity crashed my meeting, jumped my bones and left me the key to her locker - And this is why." Jack took a slim brushed-steel tube from his pocket and handed it to Dr. Smith. "It's a data-chip, but it can't be read without its owner's fingerprint. I'm guessing you have access to the appropriate finger."

They picked up Dr. Smith's laptop from her office and made their way down to the morgue, where contact with Matilda's finger did indeed bring the chip to life.

They both stared at the screen. silent in their shock as they scrolled through the document.

"Is this what I think it is?" asked Jack.

"Well, obviously I don't know for certain what you think it is, but probably. It's The Evil Overlord List."

"This is supposed to by a myth."

"Oh good grief, look at this one. *'Trooper uniforms should not conceal the face. It is also good practice for personnel to be familiar with their colleagues, so they can spot impostors easily.'* There's more of them. Lists and lists of instructions for villains. If this information gets out Storyland could be a much darker place."

"It's not just that, Jack. This is the Black Hat Society's manifesto. It's proof that they exist. It changes everything."

"I know," said Jack. "Get this in front of Foley, and don't tell anyone you've read it."

"What will you do?"

"Someone will want to talk to me I expect, so I'll go where she'll expect me to turn up."

"And where's that?"

"Where do the lost and lonely people go?"

People came to Narrative City for many different reasons. They came from the feudal kingdoms of the east, looking for a better life with decent medical care and fewer marauding orc tribes. They came from the brutal, teeming arcologies of the west, looking for a better life with more open space and fewer casual murders. They came from the rugged mountains of the north, looking for a place where silver was just a pretty metal and the dead didn't suck so much, and they came from the exotic islands of the south in search of non-shivering timbers and a decent cup of tea. But wherever they came from, and whoever they were, almost all of them were hoping to find their story. The one where they were the hero. And those destined to star in a certain kind of story eventually found themselves on Lover's Lane, whether they liked it or not.

Jack wrapped his hands around a steaming mug of hot chocolate and took a scalding sip. Costas, the cafe's owner, had left this table out just for Jack. A damp, freezing mist was gathering over the cobbles of Valentine Square, where the Lane either began or ended depending on your point of view. Somewhere close, lost in the gathering darkness, a lonely saxophone bled the blues in twelve bars. She emerged out of the mist, heels clicking on the cobbles as she approached.

She looked very different. She now had straight black hair, pale skin, dark eyes, and a power suit straight out of an office in the heights of Little Tokyo, but it was definitely the same woman.

"We'll have to stop meeting like this," she said sitting down next to him.

"Given where we are, doesn't that tell you something?"

"I'm not nearly predatory enough for you, Jackie boy."

"Oh I don't believe that for a moment. I have the contents of Georgia's locker. Foley will be reading it right now."

"And, apart from the obvious, what do you want from me?"

"Who killed Georgia and her brother?"

This earned him another raised eyebrow. He smiled as he felt his body respond.

"They were trying to sell something incredibly dangerous, Jack, surely you get that. My employers would prefer it if that document remained a myth, and so would every sane person in Storyland."

"Murder is still a crime."

"But it isn't murder when the good guys do it. Look, Jack, we prevented the sale and we put the document into safe hands. And now you and the tenacious little men of the NCPD will close down your investigation."

"I can't promise anything of the kind."

"But I can, Jack. My employers have connections in very high places. You'll have your badge back by morning, but you will not pursue this matter any further or your story will be over. For good this time."

"Who are you?" he asked, exasperation finally getting the better of him.

"I'm the woman who walked out of the mist as you waited on Lover's Lane. Other than that … well you're the famous detective. Find me, Jack Nightfall." She paused and leaned in to kiss him. It was a long, slow kiss of the kind that promised, if not a happy ending, then at least a memorable interlude. "Catch me if you can," she whispered, lips brushing his ear and sending shivers down his spine. By the time he'd opened his eyes she was disappearing back into the mist.

Jack smiled to himself as he finished his chocolate and listened to the sounds of the urban life happening around him. What a city this was. What a life to live.

"I'm Jack," he said to himself, "And I'm a detective."

Karl closed his eyes and placed his hands behind his head. Above this small stand of palm trees, a gull cried in alarm as it gave up its catch to a frigate bird. There was a small colony of them, probably nesting in the centre of the island. He felt a strange kinship with the frigates. They were pirates, just like him.

Further down the beach, members of Karl's crew were dragging their boats up through the surf. He smiled to himself as their salty banter reached him through the strangely still sea air. They were excited and in high spirits. After months at sea they were heading ashore to explore an uncharted island in search of food and water, and … well who knew what else they might find? This was the Eastern Ocean, and they were stranded among the Forgotten Isles. Potential adventure lurked under every rock on some of these little islands. He lifted his head, blinking in the fierce sunlight, and scanned the approaching pirates for red shirts. Having reassured himself that everyone was appropriately dressed, he let his head fall back and reached up and left for his fruit cocktail.

"Pieces of nine!" croaked his parrot from her perch in the palm above him.

"You always did like to exaggerate," he said, sitting up. She fluttered down to take her customary place on his shoulder.

"One does what one can to amuse and entertain," she said. "I'm surprised you're not more concerned."

"What about? So there's no wind and the back-up engine is not working. I'm not surprised; you know how unreliable western tech gets out here, particularly this far east. The Doc says he can get it working in a few days and I have no doubt that's what he'll do. In the mean time this island has already supplied us with enough food and fresh water to sustain us, and to replenish our stocks for the voyage home. Why should I worry?"

"Well, for a start the rum is gone."

"Polly, please," said Karl with a dismissive gesture, "The rum is always gone, and no-one ever knows why. Anything else?"

"There's going to be a story."

"Yes, that's why I'm sending the lads exploring."

"That's a little reckless, don't you think?"

"Not really. I'm hoping that Joe and his boys will run into something. If there's a tribe of love-starved amazons or a magic pixie that farts rainbows and grants wishes, those boys will make a mess of the plot before it starts. Meanwhile, Bates and Stains are rowing round the island with orders to take care of any stray plot-hooks that are roaming around."

'It won't work, trust me. We are stranded on an apparently idyllic deserted island, Captain. Do you honestly think the universe has just decided to give us all a nice beach holiday? No, when a voyage is interrupted like this it's because something unexpected is going to happen. This island will be the setting for a story - you mark my words."

As he made his way back to the Broken Heart, Karl had to admit that Polly was probably right. This island chain, had never failed to entertain them, and while it all tended to work out in the end stories could do untold damage to one's plans, and they were often dangerous, even deadly. He knew that the measures he had taken would not protect them. All he'd really done was put capable people in harm's way, in the hope that they could cope with it. There had to be more he could do. He left Polly in his cabin, messily devouring a pineapple, and made his way over to the figurehead. She was looking out over the beach, watching the crew as they made camp on the tree line, her red hair blowing, as ever, in an imaginary wind.

"How are you feeling?" he asked.

She twisted at the waist so she could see him. "Better," she said, "though it is strange to have the engine disconnected. It is not often used, but it is still part of me. There is a hollow feeling, where it used to be."

"I'm sure the Doc will have it working again soon."

"Of course he will," she said. "You are worried about something, my captain. What is it?"

"Being stranded here on an unknown island. Polly believes we are about to experience a story."

"I thought we were in one already. What about the voyage?"

"The search for Captain Green-Beard's treasure cannot continue until the weather changes or your engine is repaired, and these are the Forgotten Isles."

"Ah. And you are concerned about what we may lose as the sub-plot plays itself out."

"Exactly."

"Then perhaps, if we cannot avoid it, we should embrace it. Maybe then we can decide what kind of story it will be."

Roger, the cabin boy, sat by the fire on the wide, white beach, sipping a fruit cocktail from half a coconut, as around him the rest of the crew celebrated their triumph while gambling in a complex game of strategy and chance. Now it was dark, the island seemed much more forbidding to Roger, but his crew mates were still in high spirits after their adventure and he wasn't about to let them see his fear.

"So what did you do with your third wish, eh guys?" asked Roger.

Joe, placed a card on the blanket that was serving as a playing surface and rolled the dice. "it ended the same way it always does," he said. "The never-ending rum bottle made us all … incompetent and the sexy dancing ladies got all upset about it. In the end we got fed up with their nagging and used the last wish to get rid of em. They took the bottle with em when they disappeared as well."

"They left behind these little bars o' chocolate-covered coconut, though. Reckon they'd go really well at home," said Sparky, popping another one in his mouth. "Oh come on, Joe that's the fourth time you've played the mermaid queen! If you're gonna cheat at least try to hide it!"

"S'not my fault the decks got all mixed up. If I was cheating Greg wouldn't have all my money would he?"

"Didn't say you were any good at it," muttered Sparky, playing the seven of ships. He rolled the dice, swore and dropped another coin in the centre. "Hey Roger, why don't you join us?"

"Because last time he cleaned us out and you threatened to hang him from the main mast by his wossname," said Greg. "You woulda done it too, if the ship hadn't woken the cap'n."

"I've apologised to the lad since then, we're friends now."

"Whaddya say Roge? You wanna play?"

"Ain't got no money," he said. "when d'you think old Stormy's gonna let me go on an adventure with you lot?"

"When you're older," said Greg

"When you're bigger," said Sparky

"When you're smarter," said Joe. "And he's 'Captain Stormcrow' to you, 'an anyone else who ain't earned their damn stripes, ok lad?"

"Yessir," said Roger, hanging his head, certain he was about to be sent away. Instead, Joe took a few coins from the pile in front of him and handed them to Roger. "Now deal yourself in an' let's see if you can win some of my cash back off Greg, yeah?"

Karl personally supervised as young Roger was dug out of the beach. Ordinarily he would have the three idiots who buried him up to his neck out here digging, but his first mate had advised against it. Apparently there was something going on here that may need kid gloves rather than steel boots. It was certainly unusual for the crew to turn on each other like this. There was often a good deal of tension and physical humour between them, they were pirates after all, but this kind of thing almost never happened, and it was dangerous. These men relied on each other as they took on whatever Storyland's oceans could throw at them. He couldn't have them burying their crew mates on uncharted beaches.

The first mate was, at this moment, making his way across the beach, presumably having interviewed the miscreants. Karl waited patiently as the old man puffed and hobbled his way over the sand, all the while sweating under his enormous grey beard.

"Yoko Geri!" Karl said as he approached. "What can I do for you?"

"Well, Captain," said Yoko, still trying to get his breath back, "first of all, I found these beans in a small cup on your desk. I have no idea where they might have come from."

Karl took the beans and examined them carefully.

"Just as I thought. These are from a giant beanstalk. You see these black markings here? Very distinctive."

"Should I throw them overboard, sir?"

"Good lord, no. Burn them, Yoko. Make sure nothing remains. What have you found out about Roger's predicament?"

"it was as we thought. They were gambling and the kid cleaned em out - with what might be called 'embarassin' ease'."

"What was the game?"

"Shiver Me Timbers, sir."

"Wasn't that the game that nearly got young Roger tied up by his-"

"I believe so, sir."

"I expect they're claiming he cheated?"

"They are, sir. Of course this is a game invented by pirates and played for money. Cheatin' is sorta built into it. But from what I knows of young Roger, I expect he was playin' it straight, sir. I think that's probably why it upset them so much when he won."

"I see," said Karl, slightly distracted as an idea began to form.

"What shall I do with 'em, sir?"

"They may go back to their duties, Yoko."

"Really, sir?"

"Yes. They did a first class job of dealing with that magic lamp."

"They got drunk and conjured up a troop of dancing girls. They'd still be in the forest gettin' their rocks off if it hadn't all gone wrong."

"On this occasion I'm not worried about their motives. They stopped a potentially dangerous story right in its tracks. There is no sign of this lamp, or the creature that lives in it and my ship and crew are the same shape and species as they were when we arrived. For that they are to be commended. Tell them that's why I'm letting them off, and as soon as young Roger is well enough send him to see me."

"Certainly, sir."

"Get it done, Yoko."

Roger knocked and entered, bare feet silent on the smooth planks of The Broken Heart. He felt incredibly small and vulnerable, and he had no real idea why he was here. Captain Stormcrow was sitting in his chair by the small glass window at the stern. He looked up from his book.

"Ah, Roger, thank you for coming. Do sit down."

Roger looked around in a kind of blind panic, before diving for a chair and perching on the edge of it. "Thank you, sir." he muttered.

"Roger, there is no need to be so nervous. You are not in any trouble."

"Not sure about that, sir."

"Excuse me?" said the Captain.

Roger steeled himself, wondering if he was really angry enough to say this, but he had heard that Stormcrow valued honesty in a sailor. "Think I might be in trouble, sir. Think I might be stuck on a desert island with a ship fulla pirates, sir."

"But you're one of us, Roger."

Roger hesitated. "I'm very grateful for you takin' me in, sir, but I ain't one of you, not yet. I'm a skivvy what gets buried in the beach for winning at cards."

"Nobody wanted to hurt you, Roger."

"Tell that to someone what ain't spent last night screaming to keep the crabs away. Beggin' your pardon, sir."

"No, no I understand. You were treated very badly. But do you know why?"

"Because they is 'orrible, pea brained bullies what is not fit to kiss my -"

"Now Roger that kind of attitude won't get you anywhere," said Stormcrow sternly. "They were angry because you humiliated them, not because you won. Believe me I get it. They're all stronger than you; they have all the status and experience. So when you get the chance to prove that you're cleverer than they are it's difficult to resist. But did you consider that you could have won without making it look so easy? Did you think about what happens the next time those three decide to play a game?"

"So you think it was ok for them to bury me, sir?"

"Of course not! But that doesn't mean we can't understand why they did. Now, can you explain how you won?"

"S'all about probability, sir. Read about it from a book Agro stole in Aramine. He was gonna eat it but I swapped it for an egg butty, sir."

"It's a complex game. There are a lot of variables. How did you account for that?"

"You can't control the dice, sir, but if you get the cards right they'll only lose it for you once in a while, even if the other guys is good enough to take advantage."

"I see."

"Erm ... was that right, sir?"

"I dare say it probably was, lad, but you have to remember to play the game, not just the cards and the dice. If you destroy your opponents, take all their money and leave them no hope of ever winning, they may or may not bury you in the sand, but they will certainly not invite you to join them again. The real skill is to allow them to enjoy themselves as you take some of their money. Do you understand?"

"I think so, sir."

"We're going to have a contest, Roger. A Timbers tournament, to keep us all occupied and out of trouble while the Doc completes his repairs. I want you to prove something to me. You see I know that you understand numbers, and weather and tides. I know we can teach you to sail and to fight, and to lie and cheat and win. What I don't know is if you can understand people. I want to know if you can take a man's money and leave him laughing. I want to see if you can get out of your own head, and into theirs. Can you do that Roger?"

Roger had his doubts but he did not voice them. "I will try, sir," was all he said.

Karl wanted as many pirates as possible to be occupied with the contest until the ship was ready to leave, in order to give them the smallest opportunity to trip over a story and make a mess of everything. The Doc had told him - or more accurately he had screamed from the depths of his shadowy domain in the bowels of the ship - that he expected to have the engine running in about thirty six hours, so Karl planned around a timeframe of two days, reasoning that they could conclude the competition at sea if they had to. His announcement was met with predictable enthusiasm. The opportunity for officially sanctioned gambling was not to be missed, and the whole crew were savvy enough to know that "sitting around waiting for something to happen" was not a very clever idea.

If this crew had a special talent, apart from "grand theft nautical" of course, it was organising a piss-up, even when there wasn't a brewery within a thousand miles, and even though the rum was always gone. Cook and his two wraith-like, photophobic minions had set up a field kitchen on the beach and were busily performing the same magic they usually reserved for the privacy of the Heart's galley - namely turning whatever rubbish was to hand into a varied and nutritious feast. They'd also set up something of a fruit juice factory, and they had obtained a supply of alcohol from somewhere, though as with most of their work it was wise not to ask what it was made of. The resulting punch had quite a bite. Karl thought it would be better for the addition of some watermelon, but then most things were, in his experience.

Karl had put up a bottle of antique brandy as first prize, and Yoko had generously donated his last two boxes of chocolate-covered raisins for second and third. Again this news had been met with great enthusiasm. For men who were famous for their violent avarice, the Broken Heart's crew had surprisingly simple tastes.

They set up the tables on the beach, between the kitchen and the surf, so the ship could see the action and talk to the crew, since she needed a distraction more than any of them. Agro, who was quite aware of where his strengths were, opted not to enter the contest and instead had organised some peripheral gambling opportunities in the form of more physical games, until Yoko broke up the rock-catching contest on the grounds that every sailor needed at least one working wrist. By all accounts Agro was also responsible for the large, scaled beast currently rotating slowly on a spit in pride of place at the front of the kitchen. Cook said he expected it to taste like chicken.

All in all, thought Karl, it was shaping up to be a rousing success, but they would have to start the game soon, before the party got out of hand.

"You think you're very clever, don't you?" said Polly as she landed on his shoulder.

"I know I am," he said.

"So what makes you think this 'contest' will turn into a story? The crew play this game all the time, often for much higher stakes than this."

"Well," said Karl, letting his eyes linger on Roger as he helped himself to some of Cook's special punch. "The stakes are higher than you might think, at least for our young hero."

Polly let out a long, harsh call that Karl recognised as her laugh. "Yes. Yes indeed, Captain. That might just work."

Roger suspected the captain had arranged to seat him with Joe, Sparky and Greg for his first game. It was just too inconvenient to be a co-incidence. The atmosphere was chilly as he took his seat and laid his tokens out on the rough wooden board.

"Afternoon, Roger," said Joe, shuffling the cards and beginning to deal.

"Hi!" said Roger, forcing a grin. He knew he could win here, but that wasn't the point. "Look fellas, give it your best game today ok? I don't wanna sleep in the beach again y'know?" It was a bad joke but they all laughed, and the tension level dropped just a little.

Greg, who was busy constructing an army of soggy roll-ups and stacking them up at the corner of the table said, "We're sorry, kid. It was a bad thing what we did."

Roger looked each one of them in the eye for the first time since he'd been dug out of the sand and he saw that they meant it.

"S'ok," he said, "we're pirates. We're supposed to do bad things, right?"

"But not to each other," said Sparky, clapping him on the shoulder. "You're the cleverest one of us, Roger. Reckon if anyone here has a chance at that brandy, it's you."

Roger heard the unspoken question and felt his grin broaden.

"Ain't no fun drinkin' alone, is it?"

And with that said, the game began. It was surprisingly easy to keep himself just ahead of them, occasionally even dropping behind, to much whooping, laughing and the odd "arrgghh" from his opponents. He discovered that playing the players was just as easy as playing the cards and dice, only with slightly different tools. The mechanism of the game, with its complex rhythms and mathematical relationships, fell into the back of his mind as he concentrated on the men at the table, trying to discern how they were feeling and what they were thinking. Before long he found he could almost trace the movement of the cards around the table by reading expressions and listening to the tone of the disgraceful stories they told as they played. These men had been part of his life for as long as he cold remember, and he knew them a good deal better than he'd thought. He found that he could lift a losing man or install caution into someone holding a winning hand by choosing the right joke, or making the right expression as he drew a card. He wondered if this was how the captain felt all the time.

By the time he had all the counters in his pile the pirates were congratulating him and drinking to his luck, as if they were claiming part of his victory for themselves, rather than feeling the pain of defeat.

He took his winnings to the next table, where three of the other first round winners were setting up for the second game. This game went pretty much the same way, and as the sun sank into the ocean he was carried back to the ship on their shoulders where they drank liberally to Roger, his mad skills and his ready wit.

As he finally made his way towards his bunk, he heard the distinctive click of the captain's boots on the deck. He shook his head, trying to clear out the fog of too much drink and not enough sleep, before what he knew would be another demanding conversation.

"Quite the victory, young Roger," said Captain Stormcrow as he caught up. "I expect you want to sleep, but walk with me a moment first, would you?"

"Of course, sir," said Roger, falling in beside the captain. They walked to the bow, where the figurehead was waiting, red hair blowing around her as she clutched a stylised broken heart in her arms.

When she spoke her voice reverberated up through her planks, making his bare feet tingle.

"Roger. You did very well today, congratulations."

"Yes, Roger, very well done. I think you've proved that you have what it takes," said the captain.

"What it takes to do what, sir?" asked Roger.

"To really become a part of this crew, and eventually to lead them."

"What are you saying, Captain?" said Roger, almost backing away.

"For now, I'm just saying that I'd like you to take on more responsibility, and we'll see where it leads, but first there is one more thing I need you to prove."

"Yes, sir?"

"Well, you've shown us that you can keep your comrades on side as you do what you want to do. Now I want you to show me that you can do what must be done. Show me that you are aware of and committed to the needs of the ship."

"I'm not sure what you mean, sir."

"I'm sure it will come to you, Roger," said the Broken Heart. "When the time comes, I have no doubt that you'll know what to do."

"Erm ... thank you. I think. I'm sorry, sir, but I've had more to drink than any boy should have before taking career advice from an armed criminal and his talking ship."

The captain threw back his head and laughed, clapping Roger on the shoulder. "Understood, Roger. You go get some sleep. We'll see you in the morning."

The table for the final game was set up on the main deck, where the whole crew could gather round and watch. As soon as he saw the arrangement, Roger knew this game would be different. In this game he wouldn't be playing the players, but the crowd. He had not slept very well in the end. The cryptic advice the ship and her captain had given him raced round and round in his mind, leaving him sleepless and frustrated.

In the end he decided to concentrate on the game, and consider the "needs of the ship" if and when it came up. His opponents this time were two-time winners, just like him and it was safe to assume they knew their way around this game. Bates, the ship's weapon master, fresh from his adventures circumnavigating the island, was probably the most difficult prospect. He was almost universally disliked, since every pirate on the Heart had endured months of painful drilling under his harsh gaze, and he was almost universally respected because every pirate on the Heart had survived in combat because of those drills. He was virtually unreadable behind that enormous moustache, and his nerves were made of something much harder than steel.

Jash Simpson had won the second spot, a shock of bright red hair over an easy smile. He was sharper than the captain's cutlass and faster than a summer storm, but he was readable, and Roger thought he could take him if the game went his way.

The third seat belonged to a complete unknown quantity, one of the kitchen wraiths, known only as Keith as far as Roger knew, and only ever glimpsed as a pallid face above a ladle and some impossible feat of extreme cookery. Roger could only hope he could find a way to read a stranger as well as he'd read his friends.

The crew cheered them all as they took their seats. Of course their idea of "cheering" was shouting "arrgghh!", stamping their feet and throwing stuff, but at least the mood was generally welcoming and nothing they threw had what Roger would call a proper blade. The noise died down as the captain took the floor and held up his hands for silence.

"Well, boys, it's been a thrilling contest so far, and good natured too, with a bare minimum of cheating and no bloodshed as far as I could tell. Everyone who played the game deserves many congratulations, for a thing well and fairly done. This is the final game, places to be decided by the order in which the players run out of chips, last man standing to be declared the winner! Let's get it done, boys - Mr. Agro has the book!"

The table became a little island of quiet among the braying mob as the pirates scrambled to get their bets in, and in their little bubble of calm, the four contestants began to play. Nothing much happened for the first few hands, as the players felt each other out. Gone was the easy banter of the previous rounds; here they spoke softly when they needed to and not at all where possible. The first clash came twenty minutes in, when Bates and Jash got caught in an escalating spiral of betting, and neither proved willing to back down. Roger ducked out of the hand early, and Keith flashed his secretive little smile and followed suit. It soon became clear, to Roger at least, that Jash was instigating the confrontation, possibly in the knowledge that the Weapons Master would be unwilling to fold. It was working as well, and by the third time Bates was nearly out of tokens and still facing off with diamond hard resolve. It was Keith who finished him off, playing the Ghost Ship with an apologetic click of his tongue and rolling a triple six to boot. Bates bowed out with considerable grace, congratulating Jash on a game well played. He left the table to join the crowd of spectators.

For the next few hours, Roger slowly chipped away at Jash's lead until, without warning, the young sailor pushed all his tokens into the middle of the table. He smiled at roger with the same lazy complacency that had driven Bates insane, and Roger returned his smile.

"Take him, Roger!" shouted someone from the crowd, causing predictable uproar once again. It seemed a considerable number of pirates had bet on Jash to win. Roger took a deep breath to calm himself and took a moment to watch Jash. His nervousness was well hidden, only visible in the twitching of his sculpted biceps and the tapping of his fingers.

"You must have some cards over there," said Roger, breaking the silence.

Jash shrugged. "Either that or I fancy chocolate more'n brandy," he said.

Roger matched his bet, played the nine of daggers and rolled a total of seven. Keith considered for just a few seconds before he folded. Jash played the king of sharks, and Roger topped it with the ace. Jash shook both their hands and left the table, still smiling, to raucous cheers from his comrades in the crowd.

That left two players, Roger and Keith, with Roger in the lead. However Keith seemed obstinately unwilling to capitulate. He won the next five hands, and with each one the crew grew quieter, the atmosphere more charged, and slowly it dawned on Roger what the captain had meant by "the good of the ship". As he looked around the crowd he saw many men he knew, many men he could count on in a tight spot. But Keith had exactly two - his fellow kitchen wraith and the cook himself. If Roger won, that wouldn't change and this lad's razor sharp mind would remain an untapped resource. But a man could buy a lot of good will on a pirate ship with a bottle of antique brandy. That was what was best; an exciting finish followed by a surprise victory for the unknown underdog. He'd have to make it look good though.

Roger watched from a quiet corner as the hero's prize was put to its intended purpose with another colourful toast. Keith was having the time of his life, a big, broad grin on his sallow face, already more a part of the crew than he had been since he came aboard.

The captain appeared from behind Roger and placed a hand on his shoulder. Roger looked up to see him looking back, a strange look in his calm, steady stare.

"A fine result, don't you think?" he said. "And only a small amount of cheating."

"I didn't see any, sir," said Roger.

"No, but you did some, towards the end. It was well done, boy."

"Thank you, sir," said Roger, beaming. As he said it, the dull clack-clack-clack of the emergency engine ripped into the night, the sails filled and Yoko strode onto the deck, bellowing orders.

"Take the helm, lad," the captain told him. "We have a treasure to find."

4
MOON OVER GRISTLE STREET
BY INDIGO DYLIS

The Gristle Street Estate, the part of fabled Narrative City where life was cheap, silver was expensive and a jar with a living brain in would cost you around twenty dollars, depending of course on who its previous owner had been. It was also a place where an unemployed accountant might come in search of a more interesting life.

I wrapped my knuckles smartly against the dark wood door of the Wallflower Guesthouse, hoping that Alison would answer even at this late hour. The door was barred from the inside, so my key wouldn't work. I knew that Mrs. Watson, the landlady, was visiting family in the mountains, leaving the place in the capable hands of her daughter, the unrequited love of my life. To my great relief a gas lamp was lit in the main bar and she slid the spy-panel back and set one bleary eye to it.

"Oh for heaven's sake, Anthony, what are you doing on the street at this time? I thought you were staying away." she said, opening the door and dragging me in. She hustled the door closed and turned the key with desperate haste.

"Well, y'know, the city never sleeps."

"Maybe but around here sensible people bar their doors at dusk. Are you tired of life, Tony?" she asked as she turned round, looking unfairly magnificent in her simple cotton nightgown. She froze, brushed her coal-black hair away from her eyes, and swore. "Why are you holding your arm like that?"

I sat down on a barstool and flexed my fingers, wincing at the pain as the wound in my forearm screamed. Al took the stool next to me.

"Look, you're going to have to start talking. You know what this looks like, I suppose? Coming here in the small hours the day before the full moon with a suspicious wound in your arm?"

I did, of course. I knew exactly what it looked like. I was lucky she wasn't forcing expensive metal gifts on me at that very moment. The problem was that the situation was exactly as it appeared.

"I went home," I said, meaning I'd gone back to Central's bustling streets for the evening. "Been drinking with some buddies from the old firm. The wolfy people jumped me as I came back across the bridge. I have no idea why."

"Time of the month," she said through her teeth. "You're drunk. Why didn't you stay in Central tonight?"

"Nowhere to go. It was a mistake to go back there. I have nothing in common with those people anymore."

"Then you should have found a hotel or something. You're lucky to be alive."

"Probably. I only escaped because of the silver dagger you gave me at christmas. Y'know the little joke keyring? I stuck it in the blighter's face and legged it."

"Did they follow you?" she asked, sudden fear and anger making her voice hard.

"Al, I swear I wouldn't have come here if I thought they were still on my tail." I watched her nod and relax. "I just need a wolfsbane cocktail. Do you have the stuff?"

"All except the active ingredient."

"The Wallflower is out of wolfsbane? How the hell…"

"Don't take that tone with me. I'm not the idiot who crossed the Hyde Bridge after dark less than a day before the full moon."

"Al, I had to come back. Central is …. is …. it's wrong. And I live here."

She sighed and shook her head. "Well the first thing is to get you sobered up," she said, taking a tankard from behind the bar and pouring a selection of dubious looking fluids into it. She placed it on the bar in front of me and I downed it, wincing as it went to work and my head began to clear.

"I'm sorry about the wolfsbane," she said. "Mum's garden got trashed last week and the commercial growers don't bother with small places like this. I know where we can get some, but it will mean some more time on the street."

What she said made perfect sense. Wolfsbane was a cash crop in the north but it was poisonous and dangerous to handle, so demand always outstripped supply. Why go door to door when the traders at the north gate would buy everything you had for whatever you asked them for?

My vision faded out for a moment, and my head grew heavy. I rested my elbows on the bar and let my face drop into my hands. I must have nodded off because I was woken by a searing pain in my arm.

My other three limbs were tied to a surprisingly solid armchair. I strained instinctively against the copper wire holding them in place as I stared in horror at my smoking right arm, speechless with a combination of shock and pain.

Alison was carefully wrapping my arm with a clean bandage, blank faced and ignoring my reaction as she concentrated on her work. She'd changed into what I thought of as her "adventure" outfit - well worn brown leather trousers and a white shirt under a floor-length leather trench-coat.

"Wha..?" I managed.

"Silver nitrate," she said, "You fell into a lycanthropic coma and I had to bring you round."

Over the next few minutes the pain faded enough for me to regain the power of speech. "How did you know what to do?" I asked at length.

"The Big Book of Stuff Little Girls Should Know. Nan gave it to me for my eighth birthday. Bedtime reading for the badass in training." She grinned, showing a row of strong white teeth. "Now I'm afraid we have a bit of a problem."

"Y'know, I hadn't noticed."

"Yeah but I'm not sure you know exactly how much fun you've bought yourself. Y'see, the curse always climaxes at the full moon."

"If we're making that kind of movie you might want to untie me."

She rolled her eyes. "What on earth is a 'movie' and is there any chance you could grow up for long enough to save your life?"

I nodded. "Just a little joke from across the river. Sorry. Carry on."

"OK. So the curse *climaxes* at the full moon. Usually this gives the new werewolf a couple of weeks to run around howling at the moon and chaining themselves to radiators and stuff. But you only have a matter of hours before your radical change of lifestyle becomes permanent, and that means the symptoms will progress with some speed. I'd like to leave you here and go looking for the cure myself, but I'm not certain there's time."

"So that means you're going to untie me, and we'll go together, right?"

"If I'm convinced you can hold it off and not try to eat me, yes."

"And if not?"

She took a flintlock pistol from under her coat. "I complete the emergency pest control procedure," she said, voice hard. I could see in her eyes how difficult it was for her to say, and I could only guess what shooting me would do to her, gentle soul that she was at heart, but I also had no doubt that she would do it if she thought it necessary.

"As the beast takes hold of your mind you will begin to forget the little details of your life. Memories with no practical use or survival value will be discarded as your brain gets an upgrade for processing smells and sounds, as well as a host of new behavioural programs. Your mission, should you choose to accept it, is to tell me something, in graphic detail, that the beast doesn't need to know. Start talking, Tony. Start talking now."

So, tied to chair, riding a cascade of endorphins and adrenaline and trying not to fixate on the gun in Alison's hand, I told her about the day I first saw her. I told her how I left my soul-crushing job at a big Central accountancy firm and came to Gristle Street, chasing rumours of sensual adventure on the edge of darkness. I told her how I fell into a job in a little back-street guesthouse, and a cynical smile from the landlady's daughter made me want to build a different kind of life, in a different part of town. I told her how her thinly veiled contempt made my heart soar, because everyone in Narrative City knew what that meant in the long term. And then, keeping my eyes locked on her reddening face, I told her how, that very evening, emboldened by too much tequila and not enough food, I'd taken ridiculous risks with my own life in an attempt to prove I was more than a washed up accountant. I told her I could face anything if there was a chance it would change the way she looked at me.

"You're an idiot."

"Clearly, but the wolf doesn't need to know any of that, right?" I said, still holding her gaze.

"I don't date werewolves. Unpredictable mood swings, too much hair in the sink...."

"In that case I think we have a cure to find," I said, trying to keep the desperate note out of my voice.

"Yeah, I think we do," she said at length. The gun disappeared into her coat and she took out a pair of wire cutters. "But if you so much as bare your teeth at me it's high velocity silver and an improvised funeral pyre, got it?"

"Got it."

Ordinarily this neighbourhood carried on going bump well into the morning, but this close to the full moon even the fashionably dead stayed in their homes. We walked through eerily deserted streets, with only distant screams and the smell of charred meat for company, but we knew that the packs were out in force and we'd be lucky to avoid them completely. We made our way in silence, Al tense and watchful, me gritting my teeth against the pain in my jaw and my joints.

She led me back towards the River Stynx, where the Hyde Bridge lurked half-hidden in a thick, dramatic mist like a sculpture from a steampunk dinosaur park. Somewhere east of us, a woman screamed and was silenced amid bestial growls and crunching noises.

"That one was pretty close. We better move," I said.

"We'll never get anywhere if you jump at every noise."

"Where are we going?"

"The only place in Gristle Street where the unnecessary eroticism doesn't go hand in hand with the promise of ugly death."

"Ah. The Watermelon," I said, pleasantly surprised.

"Yeah. Try to contain your excitement. They don't know what 'movies' are either."

But it wasn't going to be that easy. The steadily rising, universal ache was reaching the point at which I couldn't ignore it. My feet in particular would no longer obey my instructions and I was moving forward in a kind of off-kilter shuffle. I was just about to bring this to Al's attention when an unearthly howl went up behind us. Something deep in my spinal chord leaped to attention and I threw my head back. Fortunately my jaw muscles weren't working properly and my answering howl came out as a strangled squeak. Al made an uncharacteristically hopeless sound, like a whimper with exasperated swearing underneath it. Then she pulled herself together and hustled me into an alley, fetched me a swift nudge in the back of the knee with her heel and folded me up neatly into the space behind a large iron bin.

"Stay here," she snarled, leaving me there and going back out onto the street. And so I was left alone as wave upon wave of agonising misery ripped through my body, and the woman I loved faced our nightmare on her own.

The pain built, as I shivered and screamed, until my world held nothing at all but the burning pressure building in my bones. My vision swam, then faded out, my whole body *crunched,* joints wrenching, bones grinding together, and suddenly the pain was gone, leaving me gasping with relief.

But Anthony Kessler wasn't there anymore, and someone new was driving. The new person stood up, grinned with his new mouth, ran a long tongue over his new teeth, kicked the bin out of the way with one of his new legs and loped out onto the street.

He sniffed the air and detected, underneath the enormous, unnatural stench of the River Stynx, the particular scent he was looking for. He followed it into the mist with his strangely comfortable four legged gait.

He found them struggling, elongated shadows dancing in the gas light, steel knives against teeth and claws. The new person didn't even slow down; he barrelled right into the other werewolf, biting and ripping at the oily fur, rejoicing as hot blood and torn flesh spilled down his throat and filled his mouth. He hurled the lifeless body aside and roared his triumph at the moon. A shot rang out, and something buzzed past his head at great speed. He spun around, snarling, and saw her, knives ready, big eyes wide with fear, jaw set with iron-hard determination… and I woke up.

There was none of the pain and wrenching I remembered from the outward journey. It was as if my body just deflated, shrinking back to my smaller, weaker self with a long, all over sigh. I stood there in my tattered clothes, blood dripping from my face and fingers, trying desperately not to look at the mess I'd made of the other man and holding off the gagging and puking with quiet desperation.

"You tried to shoot me," was all I could think of to say.

"I didn't know it was you."

"Fair enough. To be honest I wasn't certain myself. Why did you leave me in the alley?"

"I knew it was closing in," she said, indicating the now disturbingly human-looking corpse, "and I thought I had a better chance of stopping it if I didn't also have to carry you."

"Again that's probably fair. What next?"

"How do you feel?"

"A bit rough to be honest."

"To be expected I suppose."

"It's still in here with me, Al. We haven't got long."

"I know," she said, taking a second pistol from under her coat and pointing it at me.

"Al, I promise, we still have time," I said, holding my hands up.

"No we haven't, " she said, fighting tears. "No-one ever comes back. If you'd grown up here you'd know that."

"Come on, Alison. If you really believed all was lost you'd have shot me by now. There's a chance, and you know it."

"No-one ever comes back," she said though gritted teeth.

"But I did come back. And d'you know how? It was you, Al. I looked into your eyes and I remembered who I am. I couldn't hurt you, and the only other choice was to come back."

"Really?" she asked, desperation making it more of a squeak.

"Really. And judging by the last time, if I do change again you'll have plenty of time to shoot me as it happens."

"Ok, but you walk in front of me all the way."

"Agreed. Which way is it?"

"Yeah that's it, buddy, keep pretending you don't know," she said with a sardonic smile, pointing down the road.

The sex industry in Gristle Street has always been dominated by the vampires, but The Pierced Watermelon Hotel remained as a bastion of hope, where ordinary, living humans could exploit each other in that most time-honoured and traditional of ways, without all that messy sucking and …. well you know what I mean. As it happened I did know the way there, but only because a chartered accountant who is willing to work for barman's wages is a rare and wonderful thing for a small business owner to discover, and Ruth was extremely persuasive. I wasn't sure that Alison would understand.

By the time we stood beneath the Watermelon's red light, waiting for someone on the other side of the big heavy door to decide if it was safe to answer, I was already sweating again. With a gargantuan effort I stood as straight as possible and forced my hands and feet to uncurl. I felt their scrutiny, from a first floor window as well as from directly behind the door, as a prickle on the back of my neck.

At length a panel in the door slid open.

"Go away. We're closed until Thursday," said an agitated young woman.

"Do we look like customers?" asked Alison, tapping her foot.

There was some whispering behind the door. "What do you want?"

"My friend needs help."

"Honey, he's beyond any help we can offer."

"And if I change on your doorstep, what then?" I asked. The pain was rising at speed and I would not be able to stand up for much longer. At that moment, a yet another howl went up behind us and molotov cocktails, thrown from the first floor, lit up the street. The pack withdrew, yelping, but we all knew they'd be back before long. Our only chance was to get off the street and hope they found something else to chase.

I collapsed and slid down the wall until I was curled up in a foetal ball, every part of me filled with the icy fire that told me I was out of time.

"I'm sorry, Tony," said Al, voice shaking as she lifted her pistol.

"It's ok," I managed. "You did everything you could."

"Wait!" said a familiar voice from the window. "Young lady do not fire that weapon! Open the door, Max."

I heard the door open and someone lifted me. I heard screaming and I realised it was me but there was no way I could stop. I heard Ruth's voice again, smooth and calm, issuing urgent orders as if she was asking for more tea. I felt cool hands on my forehead, and I was vaguely aware that I made an attempt to bite them.

"Take him downstairs and put him on the massage table," she said.

"The straps won't hold him," said one of the women carrying me, "They're only for play."

"They'll be better than nothing, and maybe we won't need them. Hyacinth? Hyacinth! There you are - we need a full moon cocktail, extra wolfsbane, quick as you can."
"How much?" someone asked from the stairs above us.
"All of it. Go!"

I'm told they had quite a fight on their hands, but Ruth injected me with something extremely recreational and I missed most of the show. I woke in a big fluffy bed, my hands still secured with specialist leatherwork. I didn't blame them for their caution.
Alison was sleeping in a chair beside the bed, and she woke up when I moved.
"How are you feeling?" she asked.
"Better than I have any right to."
"That'll be the drugs."
"Ah. Did they give you the bill yet?"
She smiled. "Actually they said it's on the house. Apparently being on the payroll already makes a big difference."
"They told you about that eh?"
"Why didn't you?" she asked, raising an eyebrow.
"Because I'm in love with you and I didn't think you'd like it."
she shrugged. "Actually I'm impressed that you managed to hold out for actual money. I know what Ruth is like. Hang on, did you just say...."
"Yes, I did. Does this mean I'm not a werewolf anymore?"
"It does," she said, squeezing my hand.
"That's a relief. So how do you feel about dating accountants?"
"I don't know. I understand they can be pretty boring."
"I can't argue with that," I said, deflating.
She leaned in and kissed me on the cheek. "Boring sounds awesome to me."

5
UNTOLD STORIES
BY INDIGO DYLIS

So you want to be a hero. You want to take Storyland by the throat and carve out your own share of fame and fortune, right? Well good luck to you. No doubt the bad guys are quaking already, but before you rush off to fight the good fight, there are some things you might want to know.

1. Not everyone will be there at the end.
"Johan!" whispered Heidi for the eighth time since they picked the lock on the back door. "Johan! This isn't right! We should have met someone by now! Where are the minions?"

She had a point. They'd been prowling around the Countess Delonghi's town house for almost an hour without so much as a hunch-backed butler to slow their progress. It wasn't supposed to go this way. It had seemed like such a good idea back at the bakery, but now Johan was not so sure. Even so, it seemed foolish to turn back just because there was too little opposition.

"It's ok, we're the good guys," he said as the lock he'd been working on clicked and the door slid silently open. He smiled to reassure her as he handed her his stake and loaded his crossbow. "We have to win, it's in the rules."

Suitably emboldened, they stepped through the door into what their map told them were Katherine Delonghi's private rooms. It was the middle of the day, so she was bound to be sleeping soundly in her coffin. All they had to do was poke her with the pointy bits of wood and they would be famous heroes. Their lives would be different then. There would be no more sodding five AM starts, and no more gruelling and tedious delivery rounds that was for sure.

The door slammed shut behind them, and a single gas lamp was kindled in the darkness.

"Oh I wouldn't say you had to win," said the countess, toying with her golden hair and sipping a dark red liquid from a cut crystal tumbler. Her nightgown rustled as she stood and moved towards them.

Johan found that he couldn't move his feet. The crossbow fell from nerveless fingers. It was all he could do to remain standing under that unearthly sapphire gaze.

"But this is a story," pleaded Heidi, frozen like a statue beside him. "The leeches never win..." the words were choked off as the countess grabbed her throat.

"Silly girl," purred the vampire, "by the time the hero slays the monster, it has already become strong and infamous by killing the mere mortals who came before. This isn't the story." She clenched her fist, crushing Heidi's throat with a sickening, organic crunch and discarded her lifeless body like a soiled shirt. Then she turned her attention to Johan. "This is the untold part, before the story." Johan felt iron fingers in his hair, and a hard, cold body pressed against him. He gasped as her fangs pierced the skin at his neck.

Eventually, as his foggy mind swam towards unconsciousness, she broke off her kiss and let him fall into a soggy puddle on the black and white floor tiles.

"You're just monster food, Johan," she said. "The heroes come later."

2. Happy endings are not always guaranteed.

Alessandra Paraclete, owner and proprietor of the Lover's Lane Introduction Agency was quite surprised to find a young lady waiting for her when she opened the door to set out her sign. There was very little call for her special expertise in this town, and with quite good reason. In fact she only stayed afloat because someone left a small oak chest full of gold coins at the back door once a month. She was obviously curious about this, but she knew how to treat a gift horse and had decided to leave the man his privacy. What it meant, though, was that she didn't need to sign anyone up if they weren't the right kind of person, which was a very good thing indeed because bad things happened if the wrong people received her kind of help. She meddled with powerful forces on a daily basis. The right motives, and the right clients, were a basic necessity.

She beamed at the lady from behind her desk.

"How can we be of help, Miss…?" she asked.

"Ami Meilluer," said the stranger, looking down at her clasped hands. "I was hoping you could, y'know, help me find a man?"

Alessandra took in the sensible haircut, the short, neat nails, the practical shoes and the grey cardigan. It was likely that she could help; the signs were all there, but there were some other things to check.

"May I ask how long you've been here in Narrative City?"

"Oh I grew up here. South Central, on the border with Cape-Town."

"The reason I'm asking is that around here, most people find love when they're ready for it."

"Then what's the point of this place?" asked Ami. It was a good question, and unnecessarily direct. Quite likely indeed.

"There are some special cases. Can you tell me why you think you need help?"

"All the guys I meet end up falling for Demi."

"Demi?"

"Demoiselle Jolie. My best friend. She's tall, and blonde and … athletic," said Ami, holding her hands in front of her chest and miming a squeezing motion. That left just one more thing to check.

"And do you wish you could be like Demi?" she asked, leaning forward.

"No. I'm not changing who I am to please some guy. And I'm not interested in those meatheads anyway, always charging off on adventures and beating people up. I want someone I can count on. Someone who'll always be on my side. Maybe even someone I can rescue sometimes…" she trailed off and Alessandra took a folder from her bottom drawer.

"Then you've come to the right place," she said, turning her smile up to full beam. "You see, many dashing heroes have best friends too. Solid, dependable chaps who'll lay down their lives without blinking, just to help their people win the day. Most of them have watched their buddies get the girl so many times that they've given up looking for love, until they take a stroll down Lovers Lane and see my sign. Many would call these fellows 'side kicks'," she said, eyes sparkling, "but we know that real men don't need all the glory. Have a browse through these forms and we'll see if we can set up some dates for you." She handed the folder to Ami. "Take your time, and I'll go make us some tea."

3. The story will change you, and there is no going back.

Far to the east of Narrative City, beyond the Rugged Mountains and the Deep Forest, in the turbulent and magical kingdom of Pocosia, a young and equally turbulent monarch sat atop his horse, looking down from a high ridge. In the sleepy valley below, smoke curled into the sky from a domestic fire, and the folk of a simple farmstead toiled as they put the business of the day to bed. No doubt that fire was being used for cooking, perhaps bread, or maybe a delicious cake would be laid before the workers as they returned from an honest day's work in the fields.

"Onward," he said with a smile. "We have reached our goal."

"As you command, sire," said Rupert, captain of the Royal Guard.

An old man met them on the road, no doubt leaving his wife and children to prepare a desperate defence incase the worst was indeed happening. The King lowered the visor on his plain iron helm as they approached.

The old man moved respectfully to the side, but Rupert raised his hand bringing the column to a stop.

"We're looking for the owner of this farmstead," he said, removing his helm and dismounting. "Would that be you, sir?"

The King smiled to himself at the old man's belligerent scowl.

"It would," said the old man, warily. "You don't look like bandits."

"We're not."

"Pah! Only bandits black their shields on these roads. Real soldiers want to be known. My sons will give you a hard fight and we have nothing worth the trouble. You might as well move on."

The king made a show of counting on his fingers. "your son is ... good grief he's sixteen isn't he? And your daughters would be a prize for any bandit, would they not? But I promise, Allen of Applewood, that we are not bandits and we will not harm you. In fact your fear is a reminder of something I should have done a long time ago. Rupert, tomorrow you will visit the local sheriff and on our return to the palace you will send him everything he needs to secure these roads and make the countryside safe."

"As you will, sire."

"Allen, you have my apologies. We travel in secret, and these days I can't go anywhere without this many swords," said the king from behind his visor. "I didn't mean to frighten you."

The old man's eyes narrowed. "Who are you?"

"Your king," said Rupert.

"Nonsense!" said Allen, a slight tremble in his voice.

"Just over two decades ago, an orphaned baby boy was left in your care by a mysterious, hooded stranger," said the king. "You called him Andrew. You passed him off as your own son, made him work on your farm and kept him here until he ran away to seek adventure in the wider world. Is that not so, Allen?"

Allen squared his shoulders and looked the king right in the eye-slits, grip tightening on his staff as he fought to contain his anger.

"Aye, that's right. Everyone works around here. I played my part an' that's all. What's of it?"

King Andrew the First of Pocosia removed his helm and dismounted, before embracing the stunned old man.

"It means he owes you," he said, "more than he can say. For building the home that anchors his heart, and teaching the lessons that made him a king. Now," said Andrew, smiling through his tears, "has Mother baked today?"

"She has," said Allen, coughing the lump from his throat.

"Father, please," said Andrew. "Please tell me there's cake."

6
LOVER'S LANE
BY INDIGO DYLIS

Simon Striker, heir to a vast and powerful business empire, was widely acknowledged to be a self-centred wastrel, known for drinking, womanising and driving fast cars somewhat faster than the law permitted. He was also known, in certain circles, as a beautiful and charming young man who was regrettably not nearly as bright as his celebrated parents. Of course anyone with half a brain knew what that combination of qualities meant in this town. Simon Striker was clearly a secret identity.

"But who's?" snarled Vera, dropping her copy of Muckraker Magazine onto the coffee table and accepting a cup of tea from her friend.

"Have you considered the possibility that he's just gorgeous, rich and stupid?" asked Mary through her smug grin.

"It would be nice, but in Cape Town? How long have you lived here? And besides, talk about stamina! There's no way that body came out of an ordinary gym."

"And you realise this now? Surely it's a bit late to be putting that together?"

"I had my mind on other matters at the time, but it still means I have to dump him."

"Oh come on, Miss Venom," said Mary, sitting down and sipping her fruit tea, "You'd really prefer it if he was dumb? Pull the other one, it has a training montage tied to it."

"Look, it's been fun and everything but if he was a villain we'd know. He has to be a hero. And besides, he's invited us to spend an evening with him on Lover's Lane. Is that desperate or what?"

"Simon Striker doesn't need to use tricks like that, V. You're just frightened of falling.."

"Say the L-word and you'll be spending another night in the scorpion pit, I swear it."

"Understood," said Mary hastily, "we are not falling anywhere. Got it. Y'know I bet his folks are super as well. We could probably work out who they are, after all how many rich, gorgeous super-couples can there be?"

"Whichever caped do-gooder he happens to be, there's a good chance I'll have to kill him at some point. I don't wanna know."

Michael ducked with lightning speed, narrowly avoiding a skull-crushing blow from Simon's gloved left hand..

"You did what?" Asked Simon, lowering his guard and spitting out his gum-shield.

"I invited Jen and Mary to join us at the Lover's Lane thing tonight. Come on, you know we have to go."

"Me and Jennifer Johnson on Lover's Lane? Are you insane?"

"Come on, it's a charity event sponsored by your dad's company."

"Striker Industries only agreed to sponsor it because mum and dad met there. That doesn't exactly fill me with confidence, you know?"

"Oh in the name of .... not this again. I don't get it. Where did you get this terror of falling in love? Did you look at your folks and think 'oh no, all that happiness looks horrible. It's drunken sex with strangers for me!' Well did you?"

"You've seen some of those strangers, Mike"

"I know," said Mike, throwing his hands up, "your love of dangerous curves is legendary and yeah, I get why it's fun. But I thought you liked Jennifer."

"And that's why this is a bad idea."

"Erm, you're gonna have to explain that for me."

"Who do you know who's in love and happy?" said Vera, a challenge in her startling blue eyes.

"Well, erm ... What about your folks,"

"I suppose they were happy once, briefly. But now dad is in jail and mum spends most of her time plotting ways to break him out and get revenge. If she didn't love him she could have taken over the world eight times by now."

"Well, what about your cousin Rachel? She got married to that hero bloke, I remember the wedding. He was a proper hottie as I recall."

"Yes. She was the heir to my uncle Rang's empire. The name of Rachel the Ruthless could have been written in blood over half of the east. Kings would have bowed before her. And instead she's married with a mortgage and a little tribe of disgusting brats, she has no sex life to speak of and Uncle Rang doesn't even talk to her anymore, and all because the hero she was supposed to capture had a hot little ass and a cute smile. You're not selling this to me, Mary."

"You're right, I got nothing," said Mary, setting her tea down. "At least tell him in person. Come out tonight, let him know there's no hard feelings yes?"

Mike's fingers lost all feeling as another blow struck the focus pad. He didn't even see Simon's hand move this time.

"Everyone thinks love is all sweetness and roses but this is Narrative City," said Simon in his "patient teacher" voice launching another series of invisible blows. "Love stories are a dangerous menace to be avoided at all costs. Even when they end well they get to that ending through madness, angst and chaos. And they don't have to end well. Love stories can kill. Love is not nice, or fun, or safe. People under the influence of love are irrational, obsessive, unpredictable, dangerous and miserable most of the time. Is that what you want for me and Jen, Mike? And here I thought you were my friend."

"I am your friend, Si. I just want you to be happy, and you can't get to the happy ending without beating the bad guys y'know?"

"Bad guys I can deal with but this is something different. No love stories, Mike."

"You know we have to go."

"Ok - but I'm counting on you to watch my back ok?"

Lover's Lane wound its way in a leisurely circuit around the entire city, touching parts of every district and looming large in the lives of people far beyond the city walls.The event was to begin in Valentine Square, the spiritual home of everyone who lived and worked on The Lane. Despite its lofty reputation, the square was little more than a cobbled courtyard with a fountain in the centre. At the north end, the worlds famous Moonlit Cafe was closing for the evening. Costas, the proprietor, sat down next to Simon.

"Look at them," he said, indicating the dozen or so people gathered around the fountain. "Tourists. They have no idea about the power of this place. They just want to have an adventure, play a game and go home." He paused to light a cigar and blow a plume of smoke into the air. "This place is in all the stories, and its there for a reason. It deserves respect."

"I'm not sure what you mean," he said, watching with interest as more 'tourists' arrived. Quite a crowd was gathering at the fountain, and it looked like there would be a respectable turnout this year.

"This is where it starts, young man. This is where the magic lives. I've seen em all come. Seen em fall, seen em walk away together all doe eyed and soppy. I've seen them come back as well, happy or broken. When you come here, you let the story into your soul. Sometimes it rewards you. Sometimes it tears out your heart. This lot think it's a game - like throwing stones at the haunted house. But not you, I think. I think you know what the stakes are."

"Again I'm not..."

A low whistle from Mike caught Simon's attention and he turned to see two women emerge from the mist at the south end of the square. Mary was there in her habitual fitted business suit, both formidable and attractive in her way, but Simon didn't really see her, because next to her, striding across the cobbles with her red hair drawn back tightly from her masked face and her deadly curves displayed in purple and green spandex, was the woman he had known up to now as Jennifer Johnson.

"Vera Venom," he said, moving so he was between her and the tourists at the fountain.

"Indeed," she said impatiently, practically tapping her foot. "Oh stop it with the wounded puppy routine, you knew I wasn't a good girl."

"But ... but I didn't know you were..." the shock caught up with Simon and he stood gawping in silence.

"And now it's a stunned goldfish. Didn't know I was what? This awesome? Able to carry off an outfit like this? Too sexy for these boots? ... what?"

"Evil," said Mike.

"Less of the lip or I won't let you play with my sidekick," said Vera, shooting Mike a strained smile.

"Why now?" asked Simon, regaining the power of speech. Something in his tone cut through her act and when she answered her voice had lost its hard edge.

"Look at where we are, Simon. If we're going drinking on Lover's Lane at least one of us needs to be honest. So how about it?" she asked, making a pantomime of looking him up and down. "Which one are you?"

"I'm the one who's going to stop you hurting any of these people," snarled Simon.

"Ok I know the spandex is bold but I don't think it constitutes an actual crime," said Mary, standing between Simon and Vera. "We understood there was a charity pub crawl happening this evening. Is that not the case?"

"It is indeed!" said a man with a cheap suit, a nervous smile and a clipboard. "Ladies and gentlemen thank you very much for coming! Welcome to the annual Lover's Lane charity pub crawl. This year's festivities are in aid of the Cestus Foundation, who offer refuge, financial help and rehabilitation to the fallen victims of stories, so remember to dig deep and give generously at each of the chosen venues. Where necessary, transport between districts has been arranged so please listen up for when we're moving on and do try to stick together. We'll be moving on to our first venue," he stopped to check his clipboard "The Krypto-Night Club, in a few minutes, but we just have time for a few words from our sponsor's representative, Mr. Simon Striker!" He said, clapping Simon on the shoulder.

Simon waited for the applause to die down, mind racing, wondering what he was going to say.

"Thank you," he said, "but I'm not here to take over. I just want to say that, in addition to our usual sponsorship of this event, Striker Industries will match all donations made by you good people this evening for this very worthy cause. And now, without further a do, I'll hand you back to our capable host, and let's go get ourselves a drink!". Under cover of the enthusiastic cheering he leaned close to Mike.

"Go on with the girls. I'll follow in a few minutes."

"No way! If I'm drinking with super villains you're coming with me!"

"I will, but I have something I need to do and we can't leave those two alone with all these civilians."

Mike nodded. "Understood. Just don't be too long."

Simon watched the crowd filter out of the square and into Lover's Lane, where a fleet of taxis was waiting to spirit them away to Luthor's Gate and the welcoming embrace of the Krypto-Night Club. He took a few steps backwards and lowered himself into the chair next to Costas, who was waiting patiently, still smoking his cigar.

"Very clever, kid. Not everyone would have stuck around," said the old man.

"Well you seem to know what you're talking about, and this is your territory isn't it? So can you help?"

Costas sucked his teeth and shook his head. "Don't work like that. You gotta help yourself. What I can do is summarise the situation."

"And?"

"And you just failed the first test."

"Huh?"

"That bit just now when she gave up the powerful secret instead of messing you up when your pants were down? She was hoping you'd react a bit differently. You have been found wanting, and now it's your job to put that right."

"But she's a villain."

"Maybe back in Cape Town she is, but here on The Lane the rules are different."

"I'm not playing that game. No love stories."

"Hehe. Too late, kid, you're in one already. Think about it. You could walk away right now if you wanted, call your folks and get them to rescue your friend, never see the lady again. How does that idea strike you?"

"Ah," said Simon, sinking down further into his chair and breaking out into a cold sweat. "That sounds … awful. Damn. Any advice?"

"Well you ain't expecting hugs and cookies, which puts you ahead of most. Still, it's a powerful plot you got yourself into, and it don't need no encouragement. You can't hide from it, so don't even try. Be honest, especially with yourself, and remember for the next few hours, secrets are not your friend. Don't get involved in any convoluted schemes, definitely don't pretend to be dead and stay away from balconies if at all possible. Keep your wits about you and you might come through it with the important bits of your life intact."

"Thank you, Costas," said Simon, standing up and shaking the old man's hand. "Whatever happens, I owe you one."

"Go get her, kid."

The taxi ride to the club was more than a little strained. Mike kept checking his phone, no doubt hoping he could get one last text message off in the event that the two evil man-eaters decided it had been too long since lunch.

"So," said Mary, affecting an air of false cheer, "what does your spangly costume look like?".

Mike fought desperately to hold onto his disapproval but the grin won in the end.

"It's not spangly, it's black."

"Ooh! I know, you're that ninja guy."

"No."

"The shadow-jumper guy? He's way cool. My brother dropped him off a building once."

"Not me."

"How about that shark dude? He wore black, right?"

"Blue and white I think, and I'm not him."

"The one with the top-hat?"

"Erm, I have no idea who you mean."

"Hang on, no way! Don't tell me you're Ba…"

"Don't even say it, and no, I'm not him either."

"Hmmm. There's too many heroes wearing black. I think you should re-brand."

"It's not a brand, it's camouflage."

"Course it is," said Mary, patting his knee.

"What's wrong with Striker?" asked Vera, who had been silent up to now.

"You mean other than suddenly finding out his girlfriend's a super villain?"

"It shouldn't matter," she said, frowning under her mask.

"But it does, doesn't it? Which one of you is going to change their life? Which one of you is going to change who they are so you can be together?"

"Clearly no-one is. Clearly it's over."

Mary and Mike exchanged a worried look.

"You know that isn't true, don't you, hun?" said Mary, taking Vera's hand in hers.

"What do you mean?"

"I mean this is bound to be the first of several hilarious misunderstandings."

"No it's not. If the guy had any class or any balls he'd be here right now."

"Erm, I think he is," said Mary, gawping. The car pulled up outside the club and a far more suave and composed Simon Striker opened the door.

"Good evening, ladies," he said with a slow smile. "Welcome back to the right side of Luthor's Gate, where the laws of physics are negotiable, and everyone's tailor is completely sack-of-hammers."

"You're looking very pleased with yourself," said Mike as he helped Mary out of the taxi.

"Lemme guess," said Mary, checking her watch, "You flew here, right?"

"She likes this game," said Mike with a wink and a grin, turning to offer Vera his hand while Simon handed a bundle of notes through the driver's side window.

"In fact I did," he said, floating an inch off the ground, then landing again as the taxi drove away. He winked at Vera, who didn't respond.

"Hmmm. Mike's suit is black and you can fly… I got it, you're …"

"Can it, Mary, nobody cares," snarled Vera as she shouldered Simon out of the way and strode over to a nearby phone-box. Once she was more suitably dressed she returned, still visibly fuming. "Again with the wounded puppy-fish act. I don't know about you, Mary but I need a damn drink, you coming or what?"

It was still early in the evening and the Krypto-Night Club was not yet in full swing. A live band were busy setting up on the small stage, at least two of them bopping a along to a classic rock track that was playing on the ancient juke box in the far corner. The bar man, himself a vision of red leather and blue, gravity-defying hair, took one look at Vera's expression and started lining shot glasses up on the bar.

"What's yer poison, honey?" he asked, voice dripping with world-weary sympathy.

"Is that a bottle of synth I see behind the Vino-Calapspo in that fridge over there?"

"Ooh well spotted, sister. You really know your booze."

"I know my poison."

"Look, we could get closed down for serving that stuff outside of Little Tokyo. I was cooling it for a private party later on but you look like you could do with a lift, so I'll share it with you." He retrieved the bottle from the fridge, twisted the cap and poured four shots of the precious, scarlet liquid. He lifted one. "Cheers," he said, and threw it down his throat. Vera followed suit and the synth burned a trail to her stomach, making her shiver all over.

"Good gods that's one hell of a drink," she breathed. She looked up to find the barman already lifting the second shot. She followed suit, with similar results.

"So you wanna tell me what your deal is?" asked the barman, clearing the glass away and returning his bottle to the fridge. She turned to look at the door.

"My deal is about to arrive. Thank you," she said, allowing her scowl to soften into a sad smile, "your generosity will be reflected in the tip."

"No problem, sister. You sure you're ok?"

"You realise you work a bar on Lover's Lane, right?"

"Yeah," he grinned. "I know it's a dumb question, babe. Just wanted to give you another chance to let me help you."

"You already did," she said as she turned to face Simon who was striding across the empty dance floor. "Took your time," she said, forcing another smile.

"You gave us the slip," he said, "and this place has too many bars."

"Around here there's no such thing."

"Look," he said, taking her hand, "I'm sorry about before. It was just a bit of a shock."

"I get it, Simon, and I'm not angry with you. I shouldn't have let myself believe…"

"Yes," he said urgently, "yes you should."

"Do you have any idea how crappy love could be for us? Do you see how scary this is?"

"I do," he said. "But we can…"

"No we can't, Simon. We can't. You don't even trust me enough to tell me who you are."

"I'm…"

"Too late, Mr. Striker," she said, placing a finger on his lips. "It's way too late for that. And you were right not to trust me."

As Simon watched her walk away, the wooden door at the other end of the bar crashed open. One of the doors came off its hinges and cracked in half, showering the dance floor with jagged splinters. Mike, who appeared to be the missile with which the door's enemy had secured their victory, picked himself up, carefully dusted himself off, grinned broadly at Simon and said,

"I guessed right. She's Mary Mayhem." And with that he strode purposefully through the sundered doorway to disappear among the coloured lights and smoke in the other room.

Simon turned to the bar, intending to order something inadvisable, but the barman was gesticulating wildly in the direction of his retreating girlfriend. He nodded his thanks.

"V!" he called after her, and when she didn't stop he followed her up the stairs.

The Fifth Bar was a small, sparse affair, just a booth selling bottled beer and a few mismatched chairs in a tiny square room. But what it did have was a balcony overlooking Lover's Lane. A queue had formed outside the club, and the atmosphere on the street outside was winding up towards the good natured rowdiness the place was known for. Vera sipped her beer and leaned on the rail, a deep melancholy gripping her. Why did she care? Love was a mug's game, a terrifying menace designed to crush the unwary …

so why did she feel like this? Her thoughts were interrupted by the sound of buttons popping. She turned to see Simon discarding his torn shirt, displaying the white spandex, and the blue W on his chest. He was wearing a blue mask, and a blue and white cape flew behind him like a flag.

"I should have known. Wonder Boy. Which means your folks are Captain Awesome and Laser Girl," she said.

"Well they used to be. They're mostly retired at this point, though Mum still wears her suit on my dad's birthday." He shuddered and shook his head as if trying to dislodge something disturbing. "And I think we both know my name is Wonder *Man*."

"So it worked for them," she said as he closed the distance between them. "Falling in love?"

He shrugged. "Most of the time. Anyway, since you know my secret identity, we're all in your power now. So what are you intentions, Miss Venom?"

"I don't know."

"Then don't decide right now. Finish the pub crawl with us, and let's see where we end up."

She felt herself nod. "Ok. Guess we better find the clip-board guy before Mike and Mary completely destroy the ground floor."

"Yeah. And I better hit that phone box on the way out."

And so their tour of Lover's Lane nightspots continued as they wound their way around the city. The crowd gradually thinned as the tourists paired off and dropped out. At the Sleeping Satyr, they drank shots of 'experimental liqueur' made by students at Eastside University and Mary got thrown out for breathing fire at a waitress. Later, a sky taxi dropped them on Cloud 9, a roof-top bar in Little Tokyo where the wind whipped their hair and stole their voices, and they were showered in champagne as they danced among the clouds. They sang with a vampire rock band in Razors, near Jekyll's Gate, and Simon raced a yard of ale with one of the ladies at the Parched Watermelon in Gravestone. By the time they reached Heebie-Jeebies, the famous Central jazz bar, only the four of them remained, and the beguiling fog of adventure on The Lane had worked its insidious magic.

Somewhat worse for wear, giggling, singing and leaning on each other for support, they hit the cobbles of Valentine Square as two couples. Costas, tireless servant of the city that he was, had laid out the traditional 'survivors breakfast' and they welcomed the dawn with bacon butties and the cafe's famous 'depth charge' espresso shots.

"So," said Simon as Vera rested her head on his muscled shoulder, "have you decided yet?"

"Hmmm, I think I'm going to blackmail you into being my love slave."

"Now there's a plan," said Mary, giggling as Mike nibbled her ear.

"Seriously, guys, how do we move on from here?" asked Simon, sobering a little at the thought. He was keenly aware of Costas loitering in the cafe's doorway, listening intently.

"Well," said Mike, "Clearly we're either going to save these young ladies from their squalid life of crime, or we're going to become monstrous, evil super-villains and join them. How does one instigate a lab-accident anyway? You got a lab at home, Si?"

"S'okay you can use mine. The flying monkeys are hardly home anymore anyway," said Mary.

"No," said Vera.

"No? Just like that?"

"Not just like that, but we're not making life-changing decisions at six in the morning, in Valentine Square, after … after the night we just had." Vera pushed Simon away and stood up.

"I can't think of a better time," he said quietly. "Right now it's simple, or at least the important part of it is. Tomorrow the world will complicate it. We'll have forgotten what it feels like to be here, and we'll be afraid again. Now is the time to choose, when it's just you and your gut, and nothing else matters."

She let him take her hand and draw her close. "It was true, what I told you. I can't be trusted. I come from a long line of inventively evil scumbags."

"You don't scare me, Miss Venom."

"Are you afraid?" asked Mary.

"Nah," said Mike, "Badass chicks in lycra? Bring the thunder, that's what I say."

"There will be thunder, you mark my words. We'll show you. We'll show you all…." She felt her feet leave the ground as Simon lost himself in their kiss.

Costas closed the door with a satisfied smile and made his way over to the phone on the wall. He dialled a number and waited patiently as it rang.

"Heartbreak Hotel? …..Yeah, it's Costas. Let Florence know the pub crawl is complete, all went well and there were no fatalities this year. There are four survivors, all from Cape Town and all loved up …. you might be seeing them but I wouldn't want to call it. Reckon it could go either way."

7
DON'T LET THE SUN GO DOWN
BY ERIKA WILSON

The bright lights of Rosemary Square transformed night into garishly illuminated day, but in an alley behind the theater tickers and neon signs, darkness tagged its turf with sharply inked shadows. They cut across the body of a man lying half-in, half-out of the light, the whiteness of his crisp shirt front slowly dissolving beneath two dark red stains.

"Okay, cowboy," Lieutenant Stiles said, rocking back on his heels with his hands in his pockets. "Whaddya think?"

"Looks to me like someone got hisself shot, Lieutenant."

"While I'm sure that would pass for top-notch police-work in Gravestone, I'm afraid Captain Foley expects a bit more detail on his Homicide reports. I suggest you find some."

Danny Sundown stepped forward, watching where he put his feet. There wasn't much tracking that could be done on a paved, well-traveled surface, but he knew he was being tested. He checked the angle and position of the body, its length and the height of the bloodstains. He crouched down, taking a careful sniff. The city smells were hard to ignore, especially for someone used to the more earthy scents of sagebrush and livestock, but the fading warmth of the body helped to resurrect the ghosts of recent hours: aftershave, cigarettes, red wine, a hint of seared beef. Floating delicately above it all, a trace of perfume - attar of roses, and not the cheap dime store stuff. There was a lipstick print on the man's jaw, and smudges of makeup on his collar. Danny reached carefully into the breast pocket and pulled out two blood-stained tickets to the hottest show in town. He checked the time. Looked like they'd missed the opening curtain.

"Well?" asked Lieutenant Stiles.

"I'd say he was shot with a gun," Danny replied, getting up and moving to the alley exit. Caught in the rough edges of the brick, a clump of fur fluttered. He rubbed it between his fingers and checked the shaded tips. Silver fox. He held it to his nose - attar of roses. She'd been here.

"With those powers of observation, I can see you'll go far, Sundown. Far, far away. Tell me you've got something else?"

He saw the evening unfold - a nicely dressed couple goes to dinner, he shows her the tickets, she kisses him. It's not far to the theater, so they walk, but on the way something interrupts their night out.

"I think we may have a witness, Lieutenant. Female, height about one-sixty centimeters." He returned to the body and patted the pockets. He pulled out a mobile and remembering what Corporal Kendall had shown him about such new-fangled devices, tapped it on. Her eyes were the first thing he noticed - wide, dark, luminous. They were set in a heart-shaped face framed by chestnut hair. She was smiling and her expression drew at him, beguiling in its tender vulnerability and innocence. He was suddenly jealous of the man lying at his feet. He wondered what it would be like to have that smile directed at him.

"Very nice," Lieutenant Stiles commented, looking over his shoulder. "But what if she's not a witness? What if she's the one that shot him? Pretty girls may not kill people where you come from, cowboy, but here in Central, I assure you they do. I'll call in the description."

Danny looked at that beautiful face and knew he was as much a fool as his brothers frequently told him he was. But for some reason he was convinced that she was no murderer. She was in trouble and he had to do whatever he could to help her.

In the shadows of the alley, something moved. Danny put his hand on his gun, then saw the long gray muzzle that didn't belong to any back-alley mongrel. He rolled his eyes.

"I'll be back in a minute," he said.

"Oh, by all means, take your time, Sundown," said Stiles. "The crime scene's not going anywhere."

Danny followed the lean shape as it trotted around a corner and behind a pile of empty crates. He slipped past them and found a coyote sitting in a pool of light, grinning.

"Carlos, what'n hell are you doing here?" Danny asked.

A narrow shoulder blade lifted in the approximation of a shrug. "Delia sent me to check on you." The coyote's voice was a harsh growl and only those who'd known him as long as Danny had would understand the words.

Danny rubbed his forehead. "I know she still thinks of me as the little kid stealing food from her kitchen and getting into every kind of trouble, but I'd thought you'd allow I'm all growed up now. I don't need a babysitter."

Carlos shook his head. "I'm too fond of Delia's cooking to have her mad at me. You know how she gets." Danny gave a grudging nod. "Besides," the coyote said as he licked his chops. "The pickings out back of these restaurants are almost as good as what I get at home. And all the dogs are scared of me. They think I'm wild and dangerous." His grin widened. "I like it here."

"Well you can't stay. You don't belong. Where're you living?"

"Here and there. It's not like I need a roof over my head. The moon's not full for another three weeks. I don't have to worry about clothes and shelter until then." He pushed out his forelegs and arched his back in a luxurious stretch. "The life of an animal is footloose and free. It's only you poor humans who tie yourselves down."

"I've never won any argument with you yet, have I?" Danny sighed. "Just stay out of trouble and leave as soon as you can tell Delia that the big bad city ain't fixin' to chew me up and spit me into the nearest cuspidor."

"That's the plan."

Danny thought of something. "Heck, since you're here, you might as well be a useful nuisance." He held up the tuft of fur. "Take a whiff."

Carlos stretched out his nose and sniffed delicately. His muzzle wrinkled as he sneezed so violently he fell back on his haunches. "That's a rotten trick, Danny!" he coughed as he rubbed a paw across his nose. "What are you trying to do to me?"

"Nothin', it's just fur from a girl's coat." He waved the tuft under his own nose. "Is it the perfume? I thought it was purty."

"You don't smell it?" Carlos moved backwards until Danny put the fur away. "Humans," he snorted. "It's like you're wandering around as blind as newborn pups. There's wolfsbane on that fur."

"Don't sound like a perfume ingredient."

"It's not. It stinks, at least to anyone with a sense of smell. Its only use is a wolf repellent. Were-wolf, to be precise. If that came from a coat, no were-wolf could get within ten feet of someone wearing it without getting violently ill."

"But you didn't get that sick."

Carlos' hackles lifted. "I am a coyote that can take human form - a shape-changer from a long line of powerful totem animals and spirit guides - not a human that was careless enough to get himself bit by some crazy were. That gives me certain...advantages, whatever shape I'm in."

"Best of both worlds, eh?"

Carlos relaxed and his tongue lolled. "Yep."

"Well, if the smell is that strong, could you track it? She was at the crime scene. I need to find her."

The coyote eyed him narrowly. "I know that tone. Who is this girl? Is she in trouble, or just trouble?"

"Either way, I'm the law in these parts and it's my job to bring her in."

"All right," Carlos grudgingly agreed. "I'll follow the trail, but don't expect me to get anywhere near her until she washes that perfume off. It's like snorting a noseful of Delia's Hellfire Chili." He shuddered, stuck his muzzle in the air and cast about. "She went this way. And she was running."

"How can you tell?"

"It's like footprints. The longer the stride, the farther apart the prints. The smell is thinner here." He shook his head. "Humans."

"At least we got thumbs."

"Sometimes I think that's all you got going for you." His nose wrinkled and he backed away. "She stopped here, in that doorway." It was a deep, shadowy recess.

"Mebbe she was hiding from the shooter," mused Danny.

"Or making sure no one was following her after she killed the guy," Carlos suggested. "Don't go all soft in the head just because she gets you hard someplace else."

"Carlos!"

"What? I get just as stupid around a bitch in heat. Believe me, I understand." He sniffed around the doorway. "She headed towards the street, moving more slowly."

"She decided no one was following her." He looked at Carlos. "For whatever reason."

"Good boy." The coyote stopped at the curb, cars whizzing past. "The trail ends here."

"She may have caught a cab." There was a hotel with a doorman just to the left of the alley. "Pardon me." Danny walked over, showing his badge. "Central PD. Do you recall seeing a young woman about this tall, brown hair, wearing a silver fur coat? It wouldn't have been much more than an hour ago."

"Sure. Pretty girl. She was frantic to get a cab. I helped her flag one down."

"Do you know which company?"

"It was blue, so that would have been a Sapphire cab. You want I should call 'em for you?"

"That would be mighty helpful, thank you."

The doorman pulled out a mobile and Danny wondered if he should break down and learn how to use the dang gadgets. They did come in handy - more useful than the firehouse bell back in Gravestone for getting in touch with folk during an emergency.

The doorman handed him the phone. "The dispatcher is checking with the cabby to find out where he dropped the fare."

Danny listened to the dispatcher, then gave the phone back. "Much obliged."

"No problem. Hey, you know you should get a collar for your dog."

"He's a special agent," Danny replied. "Plainclothes undercover." The doorman laughed and went back to his post. "All right," Danny told Carlos. "We got an address."

"I'm hearing that tone again," Carlos said. "Remember, she's just as likely to be trouble as be in it."

"Gotcha pardner." Danny didn't care, he just knew he was getting closer to her.

Danny knew he should check back with the Lieutenant, but he wanted to be the one to follow this lead while the trail was still warm. He flagged down his own cab, ignoring Carlos' growls about being left behind. Danny figured the old coyote would find a way to show up when he was least expected. He always got a big kick out of surprising people.

The trail led to a shabby apartment building. It was more run-down than he would have expected for someone wearing silver fox and expensive perfume. He skulked around the door until a little old woman, puffing under the load of two large shopping bags, came up the walk.

"Excuse me, ma'am, can I help you with those?" he asked in his very best drawl.

Her sharp black eyes looked him over. "Well, you look trustworthy enough, sonny, though that isn't always much to go by. I expect if you truly wanted to mug me for my milk and eggs, there's not much I could do to prevent you, so we might as well take the chance." She piled the bags into his arms and rummaged in her purse for a key. "You're from Gravestone, aren't you? The accent is a dead giveaway."

"Yes'm, Danny Sundown from the Nothingford Ranch." He followed her through the door and down the narrow hall.

"So what brings you to Central, Danny Sundown?"

"I'm looking for someone, ma'am. A young lady." He described the girl in the photo.

"Oh, you mean Miss Talma. Very pretty girl." Those eyes raked him again. "Not here to cause trouble, are you, Mr. Sundown?"

"No'm."

"Hmph." She unlocked the door to her apartment. "When I was young I knew a Dalton Sundown from Gravestone. You look like him."

"My grandpappy. I've been told there's a resemblance."

"A mite hot-headed your grandfather, but he knew how to treat a lady." She appeared to make up her mind. "Apartment 3B. Mind your manners, now."

"Yes'm."

He handed over the bags and was up the first flight of stairs before her door had shut. He thought he heard her mutter "Hot-headed", but he was keen on the scent of his quarry. He slowed down as he approached the apartment, wondering what he was likely to find. He checked his gun, but chose not to draw it. She may have already seen one man shot this evening. Then he noticed that the door was slightly ajar. He moved to the side with the hinges and pushed it open with a toe.

"Miss Talma?" he said. "I'm Detective Sundown with the Central Police Department. I'm here to help you." The door swung wide, but there was no response. He glanced around and slipped into the apartment. On a small table in the kitchen was an open bottle of champagne and two glasses. One had lipstick marks. He recognized the shade of red. An early celebration before going out to dinner?

Tossed across the arm of a moth-eaten couch, a silver fox coat shimmered in luxurious juxtaposition. The air was redolent with the scent of roses. Danny tried to discern Carlos' wolfsbane, but he wasn't cursed with that degree of sensitivity. At least the coat proved she'd come here after the shooting. So where was she?

"Miss Talma? Please, I really am here to help." He opened the door that led to bedroom. He heard the whistle of the bat before he saw the movement, but his arm was too slow raising to block and it clipped him above the ear. The last thing he saw before the floor swooped up to kiss him was a pair of dark eyes, wide with fear and rage.

He'd found her. The light in his head switched off.

Someone was pounding loudly on the door.

It wasn't the door, it was his head. The physical pounding had been done earlier with a baseball bat. Danny lurched to his feet, clinging to the doorframe as the room spun. He focused his eyes with effort. The girl was gone. The bedroom was tossed as if she'd packed in a hurry, not intending to return. He felt as though something else was missing and reached for his gun. It wasn't there. He groaned with more than the pain in his head. First Stiles and then the Captain were going to cut him into very small pieces, shove him on a skewer, and roast him over hot coals. After the barbecue, they'd mail whatever remained back to Gravestone, where his brothers would never let him live it down. A man didn't lose his gun, especially not to a girl.

He stumbled through the living room, absently noting that the fur coat was gone. Down the stairs, past the old lady's apartment, out of the building. He didn't know where he was going, but he knew he had to find her.

"Something," he muttered, scanning the area. "Anything."

He was answered by a shrill scream and the sound of gunshots.

"Shit," he spat and set off running.

She was standing in an ill-lit car-park, a cape the color of old burgundy falling from her shoulders to her ankles. Her arms, visibly trembling, were stuck straight out, Danny's gun in her hands. A few strides away, a man faced her in a menacing crouch.

"Rosie." The man's voice was a harsh gasp. "You don't understand, please, I just want to--"

"Get away from me, Lon!" she shrilled. "You killed him! You killed Walter!"

The man straightened with a snarl. Danny saw that he'd been shot several times, but it didn't seem to be doing a lot to slow him down. He had to stop this, but he had no useful weapon. He looked around. By his feet was a battered suitcase that had broken open, clothes spilling out of it. There were several pairs of high heeled shoes, but he'd seen enough movies by now to know that throwing them at an assailant was rarely effective. Then he saw a mound of silver fur and remembered what Carlos had said.

"He deserved it!" Lon growled, a feverish light in his eye. "He took everything from me! He took you!"

"You left me, Lon!" Rose cried. "You disappeared without a word! Just…just go away, or so help me I'll--"

A soft gray cloud floated through the air and engulfed Lon. He batted at it, snarling, but choked as he inhaled the wolfsbane perfume that the fur had been soaked in. His hands curled into claws and he fought for breath. He fell to the ground, retching uncontrollably.

"Lon?" Rose said uncertainly, the gun wavering.

"I'd like that back, now, if'n you don't mind?" Danny said, stepping forward and holding out his hand. The gun swung around to point at him. He smiled gently. "I know it's been a rough night for you, Rose. Seeing Walter get shot, and people coming after you. All you want is time to think and to grieve. You need to feel safe again. I understand, believe me."

Danny knew that his words weren't important, it was how they were said - she was reacting to the assurance in his voice, the calmness of his expression. Just like taming a wild mustang, it was all in the body language. Words can deceive, but deep down we're all animals, and we know what we can trust. "I'm here to help you, Rose. I don't want anyone else to get hurt, especially you. Let me help you, please?" The arm with the gun wavered, then dropped and the beautiful, tear-stained face crumpled.

He reached out, took the gun and put a comforting arm around her shoulder. With a sob, she pressed herself against him and cried. He felt as though his heart would bust out of his chest and wrap itself around her to keep anything from hurting her ever again.

"Now now," he said gruffly, stroking her hair. It felt like silk beneath his fingers. "I need to secure our friend Lon and then we can get out of here."

She looked up at him, the sorrow in her moist eyes just about breaking him. "What will you do to him?"

He shook his head. "That's not up to me to decide. But he's dangerous."

"He didn't used to be. He was the sweetest man I ever knew. I don't know what happened."

"He became a were-wolf. You didn't know?"

An expression of horror suffused her face. "No! But how?"

Danny shrugged. "The usual way, I expect. But it does mess with the personality - makes them moody, aggressive, and as you've seen, more prone to violence."

Sobs shook her. "Oh no, oh poor Lon."

Danny didn't want to leave her. The feeling of her body against his was almost more than he could bear, yet nothing he wanted to end. But he had business to take care of. "All right, Rose, wait here." He tucked her cloak around her, though she was shivering more from reaction than cold, and walked to the crumpled silver coat. Holding out the gun, he nudged the fur, then reached down and picked it up.

There was no one there. Lon had got away.

He couldn't try to chase him down. Right now Danny had other priorities.

"C'mon," he said to Rose. "Let's get you to the station."

She shrank away. "The police station? Are you arresting me?"

"No no, nothing like that, but you're a witness in a murder case. We need your statement. And to provide protection. You may still be in danger. We can keep you safe."

She reached out, touched his arm. "All right," she said. "As long as you'll be there."

He felt as tall as a mountain. "Just try to get rid of me, Miss." He dumped the coat back in the suitcase and gathered it up under his arm. "So where were you heading before Lon showed up?"

"My...grandmother doesn't live too far away. I was hoping she'd be willing to take me in. Otherwise I would have just driven out of town. Get as far away from here as I could."

"You have a car? Which one?"

She pointed to an early model with peeling paint and bald tires. He tossed the suitcase into the back seat.

"We'll take it to the station, then."

She held out the key. "Would you? I'm still shaking."

He eyed the vehicle as one would a fractious mount. He'd only been behind the wheel of a car a few times, and never in city traffic. But how hard could it be? Certainly no worse than galloping an ill-broken horse through a stampede of furious longhorns.

"Of course, Miss. You just settle in and leave it to me."

He checked the whoa and the giddyap pedals, then got the feel of the steering rein. The transmission gave a few reluctant bucks, but he was used to that. Merging into fast-moving traffic was a little tricky, but at the round-up jamboree, Cookie would always let him take a heat or two in the chuck-wagon races. No one drove meaner or crazier than cattle-drive cooks. But even a team of racing ponies couldn't give him the kind of power thrumming through this steel-framed buggy. It was something he thought he could get used to, especially with a girl like Rose beside him. He glanced over and she returned a tremulous smile.

"I'm sorry I hit you," she said, brushing her hand softly against the lump above his ear. His skin tingled at her touch. "Does it hurt?"

He shrugged. "Not so's you'd notice." He grinned. "Good thing you swing like a girl."

She gave a breathless laugh that curled his toes. "Maybe you just have a hard head."

He nodded. "You'd not be the first to test that theory. So far my thick skull's won out." He didn't want to break the pleasant mood, but there were things he needed to know, for a variety of reasons. "So, Miss Talma, how well did you know your assailant back there - Lon?"

She shrank down in her seat and he heard her sniffle. It made him want to reach over and gather her into his lap. Not a wise notion at the moment and he gripped the wheel tighter.

"Poor Lon," she whispered. "Lon Daninsky and I were sweethearts. I met him at work. We stood next to each other on the production line and he always helped me catch up if I got behind. He took me out to dinner and to the cinema. We had wonderful times together and I thought...I thought it was getting serious. I was almost sure he was going to propose. But then he disappeared without a word. For weeks I was worried sick, until I found out that he'd been back to his apartment to pick up some things. I tried to contact him, but he wouldn't see me. He refused. I was heart-broken. I couldn't understand what had happened - why he'd changed."

"He became a were-wolf. He felt he'd be a danger to you."

"How do you know that? He looks just the same." There was anger warring with hope in her voice. Danny understood. If Lon really was a were-wolf, that would explain his reason for vanishing out of her life. He hadn't run off because he didn't love her. He'd left because he did.

"I took a gamble and the coat I threw at him showed me I was right. Your perfume, it's got wolfsbane in it. That's what made Lon collapse."

"My...how do you know so much about my perfume? Walter only gave it to me tonight, along with the fur. He didn't say anything about wolfsbane."

Danny didn't want to try and explain Carlos, so he veered onto a different trail. "Walter. He was the man who was shot and killed this evening? And you say that Lon did it?"

"Yes." Tears filled her voice. "Walter...Walter Preminger is...was my boss. He was so kind after Lon left me. He transferred me to the laboratory and let me help him with his work. He said he'd developed feelings for me. He took such good care of me. It was wonderful to have someone to lean on."

The look she gave made him drive through a red light, but he was deaf to the horns and screeching brakes behind them. The only thing that mattered was Rose. He had to protect her, she had no one else.

But he was still a lawman and something bothered him.

"So Walter gave you the perfume. He made sure the coat you were wearing was practically soaked in it. Could he have known there was wolfsbane mixed in?"

"Of course, he made it himself. We work in a perfume factory. Walter's an alchemist."

Danny ran a stop sign, thinking about what this meant. A blue light flashed behind him and a siren wailed.

Rose's face was pale, her expression confused. "Does that mean Walter made the perfume to keep Lon away? He knew he was a were-wolf? But…but how?"

"Good question, Miss Talma." He pulled in front of the police station, parking illegally. The irate squad car blocked him in. "I'm wondering that myself."

Danny got out of the vehicle and the approaching traffic cop deflated when he saw who he'd pulled over.

"Godammit, Sundown!" he said. "What were you trying to do back there? Who taught you to drive?"

"I kinda picked it up as I went," Danny answered. "And watch the language, Bobby, I got a lady with me." He went to the passenger side and opened the door for Rose.

Bobby touched his hat by way of apology. "Sorry, Miss." He glared at Danny. "Just…learn the rules of the road, Sundown, before you get into trouble even being a cop won't get you out of."

"T'aint what's done it for me so far," Danny said with a grin. "C'mon, Miss Talma, right this way."

He sat Rose at an empty desk and went to fetch her some tea. He didn't like letting her out of his sight, but she should be safe enough in a room full of police officers. Then he gave a bit more thought to some of his brother lawmen and quickened his stride. He trusted most of them with his life, but throw a girl as pretty as Rose in their midst and he decided it would be better not to test that trust for too long.

A deep voice reverberated down the hallway. "Sundown's here? He had the stones to show up?"

Danny groaned. He didn't have time for Captain Foley. Rose was waiting for her tea - in a room full of men trained to disrespect personal boundaries.

"SUNDOWN!"

At the coffee station, Danny grabbed a teabag and poured a mug of hot water. He spun and barely managed to keep the boiling water from sloshing onto the captain, who loomed over him, breathing angrily through his nostrils, reminding Danny of an intemperate bull he'd once had the misfortune to annoy.

"Howdy, Captain," Danny said. "You want to see me about something?"

"You left a crime scene!" Captain Foley roared. "You told Stiles you'd be back in a minute. That was two hours ago!"

"I was following a hot lead. There wasn't time to report back to Lieutenant Stiles."

"Not your call to make, Sundown, you're still a probationary member of the Central PD, in case you've forgotten. Things might be different where you come from. Maybe that lone wolf act plays well in the sticks, but rookie cops who pull that crap here don't last long." Captain Foley took a deep breath and his voice grew quiet, which Danny found much more unnerving than the full-throated bellow. "I took you on because Sheriff Hiram Noon spoke highly of you and I trusted his judgment. You've made me question his faith in you, but I'm willing to give him the benefit of the doubt this once.

"I appreciate that, Captain. You won't regret--"

"--That's why I'm only suspending you, instead of sending you back to Gravestone. Turn in your badge and gun to the desk sergeant. I'll let you know when you can come back and collect them."

"But I've got--"

"--I don't want to hear it, Sund--" A shrill scream came from Rose. Faster than the human eye could track, Danny crossed the room to get to her.

She was standing, staring in horror at the handcuffed man two beefy uniforms had brought in. It was Lon. At the sight of Rose, he'd snapped the handcuffs and threw the two officers against opposite walls. He stretched his arms towards the girl, growling. Danny threw the cup of scalding tea into his face, causing him to recoil, hands over his eyes, howling in pain. An entire room full of policemen jumped on him and all hell broke loose as he fought them off. Danny concentrated on keeping Rose away from flying furniture and people. Finally someone managed to unload their revolver into the enraged Lon, sending him stumbling backwards towards the window. He crashed through it and fell two stories onto the roof of a parked car. Cops pounded out the door in pursuit, but when Danny looked down, the view from the window showed only the damaged car, with no Lon.

"Will someone please explain to me what just happened!" The captain roared, blood leaking through his fingers as he covered a wound on his forearm.

A lean, compact figure detached itself from the shadows, lighting a cigarette and taking a thoughtful drag. "Sorry about that, Captain. He seemed docile enough until he caught sight of her." He pointed at Rose, curled weeping in the shelter of Danny's arms.

"I might have known you'd be involved in this, Nightfall," said the captain. With what was clearly a great effort, he gathered the shreds of his patience. "Well, Sundown? Can you explain any of this?"

"This here is Rose Talma," Sundown said. "She witnessed the homicide Stiles and I were investigating. According to her statement, that fella--" He pointed his chin at the window. "Shot and killed her companion, Walter Preminger."

"Wait," said the man called Nightfall. "Walter Preminger is dead?"

Danny was confused. "Yessir, Lon murdered him. Ain't that why you were bringing him in?"

"Nah," said Nightfall, looking Danny over with narrow gray eyes that took in a great deal but gave little away. "I just needed to ask him some questions. The handcuffs were purely a precautionary measure, him being a were-wolf and all."

"A were-wolf?" asked the Captain as he uncovered the wound on his arm. They all stared at what was clearly a bite mark. "Well, damn."

"Oh dear, I do hope I'm not interrupting anything." The voice was rich, husky, and very, very feminine. Danny felt a deep-seated shiver rise from the base of his spine to the crown of his head. There was danger here. But riding on top of that primitive sense was a reckless desire to plunge headlong towards that danger and see what happened.

In a cloud of expensive perfume and costly fabrics, a woman moved like a ghost into the light. She was all in white, which accentuated the pale porcelain of her skin. Her lips were crimson, her eyes blue and fathomless, her hair an artfully spun swirl of shimmering gold.

"Rose, my dear, how terrible all this must have been for you. Come here." She held out her hand. With a shudder, Rose left the shelter of Danny's arms to stand beside the woman.

"Excuse me, Ma'am," said Danny, resisting the urge to pull Rose back. "But who are you?"

"Why, I am this poor child's grandmother."

Danny's jaw went slack. "But you can't be!" he blurted. "You're much too…err…too young."

A hand clad in thin white kidskin lifted and patted her hair. "How sweet of you to say so, Detective. But appearances, as perhaps you should have learned by now, can deceive." Her crimson lips parted in a sultry smile, and she showed him what she was.

The blood shocked through him as all his instincts screamed at him to flee the presence of a powerful vampire, but the look in her eyes kept him frozen in place.

There was movement as the man called Nightfall shifted forward. "Why Grandma," he drawled. "What sharp teeth you have." The challenge in his tone did not go unnoticed, and the woman locked eyes with him. The air between them practically sizzled and Danny wondered how anyone could bear the cold fire of that woman's gaze.

But Nightfall did, until, with an affected little laugh, the woman turned her head to the side, bearing the slender white column of her neck. Danny recognized it as something wolves did to acknowledge submission to a more powerful opponent. He didn't know if it meant the same thing in vampire circles, but if it did…he glanced at Nightfall, catching a flare of fierce triumph in his expression before it was carefully tamped down and shielded from view.

With a cough, the Captain stepped into the fray. "I'm Captain Foley, Commander of this precinct. This young lady is a witness in a murder investigation. We need her statement."

"Yes," said the woman. "I heard about what happened. It seems no streets are safe. My poor child, such a shock." She patted Rose's shoulder, though the gesture seemed to give little comfort. "Has she not already told you what she saw?"

There was no denying the request with those eyes on him. "Yes, Ma'am," Danny said hoarsely. "She said Lon Daninsky shot Walter Preminger."

"Well then," said the woman. "The old lover attacks and kills the new one. A sad, but all too common tale. You have your work to do, capturing a dangerous murderer, and I am going to take this child home."

"I don't think that's such a good idea." Danny managed to say.

"Do you have any legal right to keep her here?" the woman asked.

Danny bit his tongue before he blurted out the charges of assaulting an officer and stealing his weapon. Locking Rose up was the last thing he wanted.

"No," the captain answered in response to Danny's silence. "But for her protection--"

The woman cut in with a laugh and gestured at the destruction that surrounded them. "I assure you, gentlemen, that I shall keep Miss Talma quite, quite safe." She produced a card and held it out to Danny. "If you have any further questions, you may contact her here." Danny took the card, careful not to brush her hand with his own, but he still felt the chill of her. She smiled and he wondered how cold her lips would feel, and how long it would take for the heat of his blood to warm them.

"Good evening, gentlemen. Come, Rose, time to go. Oh, and Captain, you really should have that arm looked at. Some bite wounds can be quite nasty." She ushered a wilted Rose out of sight.

Danny wanted to go after them, but he had no excuse. He looked at the elegant script on the card and read it out loud. "Lady Katherine, Countess DeLonghi, Gristle Street Estates."

"So that's Lady Katherine," the Captain mused. "She moves in some pretty high circles. I wonder what her connection to all this is."

"You reckon she's really Rose…Miss Talma's grandmother?" Danny asked.

The captain shrugged, wincing as the motion aggravated his bitten arm. "Vampires are people before they're vampires. They can have descendants, though inheritance issues can be sticky. But someone like Lady Katherine doesn't come down to police stations just to pick up troubled relations. There's something more. I feel it in my bones." He glanced over at Nightfall who hadn't taken his eyes off the door since Lady Katherine left. "Well, Jack? You run the Gristle Street beat. You got a hunch?"

"Your bones still know their stuff, Captain," Jack answered. "I was bringing Lon in to ask him some questions about the Alembic Perfume Factory. There've been some odd reports coming out of there. Shady employment practices, possible disappearances. It's hard to get a straight story when the current employees may have…irregularities in their documentation."

"Rose said she worked at a perfume factory with both Lon and Walter," said Danny.

Jack sniffed the air, inhaling the remnants of Lady Katherine's scent. "Will it surprise either of you to know that the Alembic Perfume Factory is owned by Lady Katherine, Countess Delonghi, of Gristle Street?"

"Right," said the captain. "Sundown, I am hereby suspending your suspension. Nightfall, the two of you are now responsible for tracking down that were-wolf and finding out why he really shot that guy. I suggest you two lone wolves learn to work together." He tossed something to Danny. It was a cell phone. "Learn to use it. That's an order." He sat down heavily in one of the few undamaged chairs. "I'm going to see if there are any good witch doctors who make house calls. I don't really look forward to spending three nights out of every month howling at the moon and peeing on lamp posts."

"Oh, I dunno Captain," said Danny. "I gotta friend who seems to like it just fine."

"Out!" growled Foley. "Or I'll bite you and see how much you like it then."

"Yessir," Danny said, and followed Jack out the door.

"So, Gravestone," his new partner said when they were standing beside the car Lon had landed on. A short trail of blood droplets pointed Northeast before drying up. Were-wolves healed very quickly. "Ever been to Gristle Street?"

"Nope. Heard some interesting stories, though."

"You shouldn't believe everything you hear."

"I don't."

"Good. 'Cause believe me, it's much, much worse."

Danny loosened his gun in its holster. "Right."

Jack's smile was slanted and humorless. "Bring it if it makes you feel better, but don't expect it to stop what we're likely to come up against."

"Might slow 'em down a bit. Sometimes that's enough." He gave a sharp whistle and the shaggy form of Carlos emerged from the darkness ahead of them. Jack made a small noise of surprise, but didn't react otherwise.

"Thought you might end up back here," Carlos said. "I've been waiting. You've had some interesting visitors."

"This is the one we're interested in," Danny said, pointing to the blood trail. "Feel up for a hunt, Buddy?"

Carlos gave a wide coyote grin. "Always," he said and set off with his nose to the ground. "You guys coming?"

"Well," said Jack as they followed. "You do have some aces up your sleeve."

"My grandpappy taught us boys how to play at cards. But it was Granny Sundown who showed us how to win."

"Remind me never to play cards with your gran."

Danny smiled and broke into a trot. The night was clear and so was the trail. Carlos wasn't the only one who was always up for a hunt. Jack laughed and moved into position beside him. Danny was still taking his measure, but it felt right having him there, especially as the twisted ruins of Jekyll's gate rose out of the darkness.

Gristle Street, dead ahead.

The darkness deepened, skeins of mist fluttered past, obscuring piles of trash and feebly twitching mounds of...other things that lay heaped in the shadows of the crumbling buildings. Voices whispered and moaned, wild laughter and shrill cries briefly punctuated the constant low-level murmuring. Echoes tricked the ear, making the voices sound safely distant, then just behind your shoulder.

Danny turned to Jack, to see how he felt about this place, but he'd disappeared. A thin, scabrous arm wrapped itself tightly around his throat and he felt a sharp-edged implement pressing against his kidney.

"Your money and your life," someone hissed in his ear.

"Ain't that supposed to be 'or'?" Danny wheezed through his constricted windpipe. The sharpness pressed deeper.

"Not on this street. Hey!" The voice cracked from a menacing baritone to an irate soprano as Danny's attacker was pried off him. "I'm working here!"

"Hyacinth," Jack said, holding up the small, stick-like figure by the scruff of the neck. "What did I tell you about mugging strange men?"

"Stab first, threaten later," Danny's attacker muttered sullenly. It was only then that Danny realized it was a girl. A very young girl, not yet into her teens. "Your friend would be missing a kidney, then."

"Serve him right for letting you get so close."

A ragged smile gleamed through the layers of dirt on her face. "Nah, nobody hears me coming."

"Okay, then don't let me hear you going," said Jack, putting her down and flipping a large coin into the air. It vanished almost as magically as she did. "And don't let your mum spend it on moon-dust!" he yelled after the retreating silence. "A good kid..." he paused. "Well, no, but she's got some decent brain cells to work with. Unlike her mother who blew them away to 'dust years ago." He punched Danny lightly in the kidney. "Still there? Right, looks like we go this way." He pointed to a bank of rancid fog where a swirl marked Carlos' vanishing tail.

They entered the miasma - a visible exhalation of the stench rising from the stagnant water oozing past the length of Gristle Street.

"The River Stynx," Jack said.

"I'll say," Danny replied.

"The trail is leading us to the docks."

"What's there?"

"All the things that make the river smell like this."

Carlos reappeared, his nose wrinkling. "It's getting a bit thick here, but I'd say he spent some time hanging around that building." He gestured with his snout towards a long, single-story warehouse with a large boat landing. The windows were too encrusted with grime to see through, but there didn't appear to be anyone home.

"Right," said Jack, picking up a broken chunk of brick. "Time for a bit of judicious B&E." With the precision of much practice, he smashed a single pane and flipped the inside catch. Pushing the open window revealed a sill as filthy as a saloon welcome mat during the rainy season. Jack grinned at Danny. "After you," he offered graciously.

Danny made a face, but placing his hands carefully, jumped over the shoulder-high sill as if he were mounting a bareback pony, and slipped over the other side.

"Well?" whispered Jack.

"Dark in here," Danny replied.

"Pull out your phone."

"Who'm I calling?"

"Not the police, they won't come here. Turn it on and use the screen as a light."

"Now how 'bout that?" Danny said, shining the small beam around. "Looks like there's a door a few meters thataway. I'll let you in."

Jack stepped inside, holding out his own phone. Carlos followed, but stopped in the doorway, ears flat against his skull. "Carlos?" Danny prompted. "In or out?"

The coyote backed away. "So much blood," he said, his voice muffled as if he were trying not to breathe. "Animals in pain. The smells...too strong. I'll...stay out here. Keep watch." He backed away, whimpering.

The warehouse was deserted, but it wasn't empty. The walls were lined with cages, hooks dangled from the rafters.

"What is this place?" Jack asked.

"Carlos said something about 'animals'," Danny answered slowly. "We do a fair bit of trappin' and skinnin' where I come from. That's what it looks like to me, on an industrial scale."

"Fur trade, okay. But what's the connection between fur and perfume? Why would Lon come here?"

"You get more than fur from animals," Danny suggested. "Lady Katherine's perfume was heavy on the animal musk. Maybe that's what gave Carlos a snootful. The raw stuff'll knock you flat."

"It's doing a good job of that now. Let's get some fresh air." They both left the warehouse, inhaling the rancid river air with relief. Jack eyed Danny. "How do you remember things like that - what sort of perfume Lady Katherine was wearing?"

"Everything she had on came from an animal," Danny said. "Her shoes and gloves were leather; her dress was cashmere; her coat, lynx fur; her jewelry was pearl and coral. Even the combs and pins in her hair were ivory, or tortoiseshell. She surrounds herself with bits of living creatures. That sort of thing sticks with me."

"Maybe she's just allergic to synthetics," Jack offered. "Ever think of that?"

"What's a 'sin-thetic'?"

"Never mind, Gravestone. So where does your furry friend say Lon went next?"

But Carlos couldn't tell. He'd been overwhelmed by the smells from the warehouse, and kept his tail tucked tightly between his hocks until they'd left it far behind. "Bad medicine," he muttered darkly. "That is a cursed place, full of terror and pain."

"Yeah," Danny agreed, looking around at the burnt-out buildings staring blindly with blank and broken windows. The despair and hopelessness were palpable. "I get what you mean, pardner."

Jack was oblivious to the surrounding blight, long ago becoming inured to it. "Let's try the perfume factory, then. We need to check out Walter's lab anyway, maybe we'll get a lead on Lon there."

"If it's away from here, I'm in favor."

"The neighborhood is slightly better. The rats are big enough to shake the kids down for their lunches, whereas here, the kids could be lunch." On cue, a lone wail drifted out of the reeking darkness and dwindled into heartbreaking sobs that no one would answer.

Danny shuddered. "Let's get the hell out of here."

"Excellent notion," Jack replied. "But I suspect these gentlemen wish to prolong our stay."

Five shadowy outlines, not all of which appeared entirely human, blocked them in. Without hesitating, Jack reached both hands into his coat. Snapping out from one hand, a collapsible baton extended to full length. In his other, something sharp and evil gleamed in the dim, greasy light. Danny's hand hovered near the revolver at his hip. The two police officers edged together until they were back-to-back, circling slowly as they sized up their opposition. The attackers drew inwards, allowing their faces to be seen. It was not an improvement. They were armed with bent pipes, homemade bludgeons, and sticks with nails in them. Unsophisticated weaponry, but nasty nonetheless.

"Would it help if I pulled out my badge?" Danny asked.

"Only if you want to stab one in the eye with it."

"Nah, the ones you guys give out don't have the nice sharp points like ours do. I'll stick with what I know best." His gun was a blur as it jumped out of its holster and he spun on his boot heels as it roared five times. Weapons flew out of five fists and clattered to the ground. Without missing a beat, new sticks, a length of chain, a broken bottle and a filthy sock filled with a brick appeared in their stead.

"Not helping," commented Jack, blade and baton flashing in short, defensive arcs. "Just shoot them. We'll figure out the paperwork later."

"Uh, I just did the math and I only got one shot left."

"Then make it count," Jack said as he blocked a two-by-four with his baton and slashed his knife across the arm that held it. A length of chain lashed out, wrapping around his baton. Jack yanked on the chain and snapped the baton down on the man's head.

Danny ducked beneath the loaded sock, and reached into his boot, unsheathing a long bowie knife. As the sock came round again he slashed the knife downwards across its trajectory. The loaded end flew free, smashing into the face of another attacker. The thug lurched into the path of a broken bottle and slid to the ground holding his stomach. A foot lashed out at Danny. He jerked away, but not before hearing the tearing of cloth and feeling a thin line of fire on his upper thigh. The man had razor-blades pushed through the tips of his shoes. A chain whistled through the air, wrapping around the thug's neck with a crack and he collapsed. Jack stepped into view.

"Thanks, Jack," Danny said. "Another swipe of that razor blade, and I'd'a had to explain to Granny Sundown about the lack of great-grandchildren." He raised his gun and blew Jack's hat off his head.

Jack stood frozen, his hand tightened on his knife and the breath hissed through his teeth. Then he looked at Danny's eyes and turned around. With a groan, a man dropped his lead pipe and fell over backwards, a hole in the center of his forehead.

"Cutting it a little close, Sundown?" Jack asked, using Danny's name for the first time. He picked up his hat and fingered the hole drilled through the center of the crown.

"Nah," Danny answered as his colt pistol spun around his finger and back into its holster. "He had a good two inches on ya."

"Hey," said Carlos, trotting up, zig-zagging through the sprawled bodies. "Are you done here yet? I found a place that throws away a great spaghetti bolognese."

Jack looked at Danny. "I could eat." He glanced down at the man curled around an oozing bottle. "No red wine, though."

"That reminds me," said Jack, pulling a flask out of his pocket. "Here, pour this on your leg. I don't want to think about what might have been on that razor blade, and I don't want to have to answer to Granny Sundown."

Danny doused the wound, exclaiming at the sting and blinking at the fumes. "What is it?"

"About eighty proof."

Danny looked at the flask and took a swig. He nodded as he swallowed. "Yep," He agreed, his voice high and hoarse as he handed it back to Jack who took his own healthy mouthful.

He clapped a hand on Danny's shoulder as Carlos led the way. "Well, partner," he said. "It's possible you might survive this case yet."

"You had doubts?" Danny asked, taking out his gun and carefully reloading it.

Jack shrugged. "It's not an easy beat. I tend to work alone because no one else lasts very long."

Danny slapped his gun back into its holster. "Well, we Sundowns ain't so easy to kill."

Jack gave him his tight, slanted smile. "I can see that." His eyes grew dark. "But keep in mind there are worse things than dying."

Danny shivered, as if someone had stepped on the place where his grave would someday be.

"Let's hit the factory first," Jack said. "It's only a few blocks." They headed north, away from the noisome stench of the river and the crumbling wreckage surrounding the Jekyll Gate. The transition was noticeable. There were working street lamps, and the roads had more cobbles than mud. Carriages appeared - most with guards riding shotgun - and there were a few pedestrians hurrying from one pool of light to the next. Evidently, even in the good neighborhoods, Gristle Street after dark was no place for the faint of heart.

"Don't look like the folk here put too much faith in the police," Danny remarked.

Jack nodded. "I can't blame them. Until recently, Central PD's standard operating procedure has been containment, rather than enforcement. For years, the best the police could do was try to keep the bad of Gristle Street from spilling out. As long as trouble stayed local, they didn't interfere."

"So what changed?"

Jack's grin was feral. "Me. I grew up here, these are *my* streets. I know what happens to the weak and unwary in these parts. I lived it."

"You still got family around?"

"Not any more." His voice was flat and bleak. "One way or another, the Street took them. It takes everyone, eventually."

"But you got out."

"Says who?" Jack replied obliquely. "The factory's over there, on the corner." The two-story brick building was dark and shuttered.

"Looks closed for the night."

"Not a lot of shift work going on - legitimate, anyway." Given the relative poshness of the neighborhood, Jack chose to pick the lock to the back door, rather than bash in another window. Carlos smelled nothing on the factory floor, though the reek of perfume caused him to sneeze repeatedly. They found the entrance to Walter Preminger's lab - it having a helpful sign with his name on it that also suggested they Keep Out - advice they chose to ignore.

"I'm in," Jack said, as the lock clicked and the door swung open. "Wow," he said as they stared at a room that had been methodically stripped bare.

"Looks like someone maybe knew we was coming."

"Freeze!" a voice shouted from behind them.

"Does that mean we should put our hands up, or keep 'em where you can see 'em?" Danny asked, peering gingerly over his shoulder at the security guard who was pointing his gun at them. "I wouldn't want there to be an unfortunate misunderstanding on that point."

Before the guard had a chance to make up his mind, a drippy-nosed Carlos landed on his back, sending him to the ground. His gun went off at the impact, the bullet whining past Jack's ear.

"I'm starting to think I need to apply mosquito repellent." Jack said. He took the gun and checked the cylinder. "Whaddya know about that? Silver bullets." He hunkered down next to the guard who was trying to breathe with six stone of coyote sitting on his spine. "Expecting a were-wolf attack? Why?"

Carlos licked the man's ear, nibbling a little at the top edge. The guard whimpered. "Dr. Preminger, he gave the bullets to me weeks ago. Said a were-wolf might show up, so I should be ready."

"Foresightful man, Dr. Preminger," Jack murmured. "Did he give the were-wolf a name?"

Carlos pressed his very cold nose against the man's neck. The guard yelped. "Lon! Lon Daninsky! Said he'd be violent and I should shoot him on sight. Said it would be for the best, all things considered."

"I doubt Lon's feelings were among those considerations," Jack commented. "There are still five bullets in here, so I take it you've not seen Mr. Daninsky?"

"No!"

"What about Dr. Preminger? When was the last time you saw him?"

"Earlier this evening, at the start of my shift. Saw him leaving."

"Was he carrying anything?"

"Leather satchel, as usual. Also a big shopping bag."

"Do you know what was in the bag?"

Carlos sneezed in the guard's hair. "Pardon me," the coyote snuffled, wiping his nose on the man's shirt.

"No! I don't know!"

"What about his lab, it's been cleaned out, do you know by who?"

The guard hesitated until Carlos snapped his teeth shut with the sound of a bear trap.

"Men! Two men came a few hours ago, carted everything away."

"You didn't try to stop them?"

"They had authorization! Signed by Dr. Preminger."

"Somehow I doubt Walter was doing any paperwork tonight." Jack said, getting to his feet. "Sundown?"

"Okay, Carlos," said Danny. "Let 'im up."

Carlos stepped off, and the guard crawled several yards away before rising to a defensive crouch. "You're not going to set him on me again?"

"Not as long as you're not shooting at us." Jack flashed his badge and a smile. "Central PD, Detectives Nightfall and Sundown."

The guard did not relax. "Police? What are you doing here?"

"Investigating a murder." He pocketed the bullets and handed the empty gun back to the guard. "Dr. Preminger was killed tonight. Is there anything else you can tell me about the men who cleared out his lab?"

"No," the guard answered, examining his gun sulkily. "I can't."

Carlos grinned. "I can."

Carlos led them swiftly through the streets, lifting his nose occasionally as if testing the air for a particular combination of scents.

"It's how he navigates," Danny explained. "Olfactory triangulation." Jack simply grunted, lost in thought. Danny wanted in on that action. "So you think the Doc was doing more than mixing perfume in his lab?"

"Yeah, I do. Why else make it all disappear before we could check it out?"

"Question is, were they cleaning up on general principal, or does it have something to do with the case?"

"Only way to find out is to find out," Jack answered. "Hey, I think your pooch has taken us on a wild pasta chase."

Carlos was standing beneath a green and white striped awning with the name "Omerta's" printed in red. His tail wagged happily. "I told you, they got the best spaghetti bolognese. I'd know it anywhere."

"The guys who cleared out the lab came from this restaurant?"

"Yep, they brought the guard some take-away."

"Lying bastard," Jack swore. "He knew who they were. Did they come back here?"

Carlos snuffled around the entrance. "I don't think so. I'd probably smell the perfume if they had." He wrinkled his nose at them. "I can still smell it on you guys."

Danny watched Jack try not to be obvious about sniffing himself. He grinned. "Don't worry, I bet you smell real purty." He gestured at the restaurant. "Do we go in?"

Jack nodded. "I know the place. It's a front for black marketeers. They've got couriers-for-hire, and provide temporary storage of illicit goods. Efficient service with no questions asked." They stepped into the foyer and the smells of toasted garlic, melted cheese, and hot sausage wrapped them in a warm embrace. "Not to mention cannoli to die for."

Two large men, whose expensive suits did not lay smoothly over the place where one might wear a shoulder holster, approached.

"Literally?" Danny asked.

Jack shrugged. "At least you know your last meal will be a good one."

"Do youse got a reservation?" one of the men asked.

"No, just this." Jack slipped his hand into his coat. The men reached quickly towards the gun-shaped lumps beneath their jackets, but relaxed when Jack pulled out his badge."Well if it ain't two of Central's finest," the talking one said. "We always got a table for our friends on da force. Just youse guys? Or will dere be more in your party?"

Danny saw a sign on the wall that said 'No shirt, No shoes, No dice', so coyotes were out. "Just us," he replied.

"Dat's fine, den." He snapped his fingers and his silent partner picked up a couple of menus. "Please to follow Guido here."

There were few other diners but Danny felt the focus of all their eyes on him, hard with suspicion. As they were seated, the low buzz of conversation fell to nothing.

"You ever git the feeling you're not welcome?" Danny whispered.

"Nope," Jack grinned. "I'm too much fun to have around. Have a breadstick." The breadsticks were the size of truncheons. Jack snapped his in two, making a sound like a gunshot. Everyone in the room flinched.

"So what are we doing here?" Danny asked after Guido had lit the candle stuck in the neck of a wax-covered bottle and gone off to loom in the doorway. Blocking the exit, Danny observed. When the door to the kitchen swung open, he noted the location of the back entrance, but the glimpse of flashing knives and wicked cleavers gave him pause.

"You said you could eat," Jack said, perusing the menu. "And for the moment, I'm out of leads. Until we find out what Walter Preminger was up to, we got nothing. Maybe we'll get lucky and those two late-night movers will show up. Mmmm, they got zabaglione."

Danny couldn't match Jack's interest. He felt uneasy, on edge. "I'm going to check on Carlos," he said, heading for the back door.

He received some dirty looks on his way through the kitchen, but the only things thrown at him were a few suggestive hand gestures. Out back, the clatter of cutlery was replaced by a peculiar melodic wheeze. Danny crept around the large trash bins and stared at the scene in the alley.

Another bottle with a candle had been placed on the ground beside an enormous bowl of spaghetti and meatballs. Carlos crouched on one side, slurping the long noodles like a pro. Across from him, a dainty cocker spaniel chewed a meatball. Above them, the chef played an accordion with solemn intensity. Carlos paused eating to nudge another meatball towards the spaniel, who licked a glob of sauce from the coyote's nose.

Something rustled behind Danny, but he assumed rats and didn't turn around. This time the blow to his head was solid and he was out before the pavement smacked him in the face.

Danny couldn't see. He opened his eyes, he still couldn't see. It was hard to breathe. There was a gag in his mouth, a blindfold around his eyes. He shifted, cautious of the pain thrumming in his head and through his joints. He was sitting in a chair, his hands cinched behind his back, his legs tied with heavy rope. He tested his bonds, they were done well - almost tight enough to cut off circulation. Wriggling his foot, he discovered the knife he kept in his boot was gone. He couldn't have reached it trussed up like this, but he'd gotten it as a present on his ninth birthday, and it upset him to lose it. He considered what else he might stand to lose.

"Awake, are you?" The voice was deep, unfamiliar, but it was accompanied by a smell of garlic and tomato sauce. Danny didn't have to have Carlos' nose to recognize a whiff of Omerta's. "Mebbe we can have a little chat. Let me help you with that." Danny felt the cold blade of a knife against his cheek as the gag was sliced off. A sting and a trickle of wetness indicated that he'd been cut. "Whoops, sorry about that. You keep your knife sharp, don't you? The blade was placed against Danny's neck, his pulse pressing his skin against the edge with every beat. He swallowed carefully.

"What did you want to talk about?" Danny asked.

"Who are you and what are you snooping around for?"

"Detective Daniel Sundown, Central PD. Homicide investigation. Who am I talking to?"

"You can call me Mr. Red."

"Mr. Ed?"

The tip of the knife pricked his neck. "Red - like the color of your blood, copper." The knife slid up under his nose, like a sharp steel mustache. "You know what I think?"

"What?"

"I think you're a nosy parker. I think you go where you aren't wanted and ask too many questions. You stick your nose into other people's business, and maybe it's time someone cut it off."

Danny braced himself for the cut of the knife into his flesh, wondering if there was any chance of rescue before he lost too many important bits.

"Mr. Red! Mr. Red!" Another voice interrupted.

"What is it, Mr. Scarlet?" answered Mr. Red. "I'm busy here."

"He found us! He already took out Mr. Crimson and Mr. Rust!"

"Find Mr. Carmine and Mr. Puce and take care of it, Mr. Scarlet. Do I have to do all the thinking here? Has Mr. Vermilion checked in yet?"

Mr. Scarlet's only response was a gasp and a moist thud. Something clattered to the floor. Danny recognized the deflating wheeze of the accordion.

"Mr. Vermilion won't be coming." Danny knew that voice. He'd heard it arguing with Rose in a car park. It was Lon Daninsky. He wasn't sure how he felt about that, but the chill of the knife left his face, so that was a plus.

"You shouldn't have come here," said Mr. Red. The room exploded in gunfire. A bullet slammed into Danny's shoulder and he tipped over backwards. He lay on the hard concrete floor, the roar of blood in his ears camouflaging the silence until he felt the hard grip of a hand around his throat.

"Where is Rose?" Lon asked.

"I...can't tell you that," Danny choked.

Lon growled, his breath burning in the cut on Danny's cheek. "You think you're protecting her, don't you? You're not. She's in danger and I have to save her." A square packet was shoved into the pocket of his coat. "Go on, keep chasing your little clues and maybe you'll figure it out. Leave Rose to me, because she's the only thing that matters. She's all I have left."

The pressure was taken from Danny's throat and he was alone, feeling the warm blood pouring from his wound with every throb of his heart, spreading out beneath his shoulder, soaking into his clothes. The pain dulled, he felt increasingly sleepy. He closed his eyes and the wheezy song of the accordion followed him into his dreams.

Danny woke up. He had no idea where he was, but he was warm, dry and alive, which was a great deal more than he had any reason to expect. Already this night was reminiscent of one long weekend he and his buddies cruised Lover's Lane. Waking up battered and exhausted in a strange location was the mark of a successful trip. He raised his eyelids to find a young woman bending over him. The memories of Lover's Lane were reinforced as she smiled at him, her lush curves not so much contained by her lace-trimmed corset as emphatically offered up for consumption. If this was some new kind of torture, he wasn't entirely averse to it.

"Well now, don't you have pretty eyes when they're open?"

"M...ma'am?" Danny's mouth was very dry, and the view wasn't helping.

"See anything you like?" She moved her shoulders to create a wave pattern across her exposed flesh that sent Danny's pulse racing at dangerous speeds, especially considering his recent blood-loss. He resented the black spots crowding before his eyes that obscured his view of the show.

"Now, Abby," said Jack from the doorway. "That's hardly fair. The man's been shot."

Abby regarded Danny with a look that would have ignited an icicle. "I've seen worse," she said. "A guy from the lumber yard sawed off his hand, and still made it to his appointment. One of the girls stitched him up so he wouldn't bleed over everything." She leaned closer to Danny until he could feel the warmth radiating from her skin. "There's nothing like a brush with death to help a man prioritize the important things in life. Isn't that true, Detective?"

"Yes'm," he agreed. With great reluctance he dragged his gaze to his partner. "Jack, what happened? Where am I? And who is this…impressive young lady?"

"Hmph." The young lady in question flounced back as Jack stepped forward. "Darn cops, always asking questions when there are so many more interesting things to do."

"Danny Sundown, this is Abyssinia Moore. She works here at the Pierced Watermelon Hotel. You're in her bed, you lucky sod."

Danny had heard of the Pierced Watermelon. Gravestone boasted many a fine brothel, but even those girls spoke in hushed whispers of quality and variety of entertainment offered by the Watermelon and the prices commanded by its most talented artists. Even if he was in any shape to partake, he doubted he'd be able to afford even the most basic rate. He glanced at the pouting Abyssinia. Perhaps they had some sort of lay-away plan…he dragged his wandering mind back to the case.

"What didja bring me here for?" he asked. "And where'd Lon go?"

"Lon?" Jack's eyebrows lifted. "So he's the one that tore the place up so bad. I shoulda guessed." He shook his head. "It took me a long time to find you, Sundown. Carlos was knocked out by a mickey slipped in his spaghetti. Sick as a…dog, he was. Sworn off pasta for life, or so he says. He was in no shape to track you. If Hyacinth hadn't come clean about her involvement, I doubt we'd be talking. You'd lost a lot of blood."

"Hyacinth? The little girl from the alley? What's she got to do with this?"

"The gang from Omerta's hired her to knock you out. She is very good at what she does. Fortunately, they welched on her payment, so she came to me with an offer I couldn't refuse. Her mother sometimes works here when she's off the 'dust, so it was her idea to bring you in through the Watermelon's VIP tunnels."

"Wait," puzzled Danny. "If the gang took out both me and Carlos, why didn't they go after you?"

Jack's grin was sharp and predatory. "Who said they didn't? Still, it took a while for the dust to settle and for me to sort through the debris and discover that you were missing. When Hyacinth finally led me to you, all we found were five dead thugs and a bunch of smashed lab equipment. Oh, that reminds me." He patted his pockets and pulled out Danny's gun, badge, and knife. "Found these on the guy next to you. Thought you might like them back." He put them on the frilly nightstand next to the bed.

"Thanks, Jack. But they look a little out of place, dontcha think?"

Abyssinia laughed. "Honey, I've got a snub-nose in the drawer, a crowbar behind the headboard and a shotgun under the bed. Ain't nothing sure in this world but what you can keep for yourself."

Danny moved his head. "Cosh under the pillow?"

Abyssinia smiled. "Very good."

There was something Danny was forgetting, something about his clothes. By the feel of the sheets against his skin, he wasn't wearing anything but the bandage on his shoulder. He didn't want to dwell on who might have undressed him, for various reasons. He closed his eyes, trying to remember what had happened after he was shot. Lon's hand on his throat, saying Rose's name, then something was shoved in his…

"Where're my clothes? My coat?"

Abyssinia made a face. "You don't want that nasty thing. Soaked in blood and full of holes. It got tossed in the bin. Probably scavenged by dogs and 'dust-heads by now."

Danny's heart sank. "Gone?"

"Abby," said Jack, "don't be cruel. I know a pocket never goes unsearched in this neighborhood."

She rolled her eyes. "All right." She reached down the front of her corset - though how anything else could possibly fit in there was an inexplicable mystery - and pulled out a square leather case. "I was only keeping it safe. You could get into such trouble bringing this in here. We got rules. You break 'em, you're out on your ass."

"What's in it?" Danny asked.

"You don't know?" Jack asked. He held out his hand and Abyssinia gave him the case.

"No, Lon put it in my pocket before he left."

"Wasn't Lon the one who shot you?" Jack said.

Danny shrugged, forgetting, and winced at the pain. "If he did, it was probably an accident. There were bullets flying everywhere. He could have killed me, but he didn't. Instead he gave me that. Said something about a clue."

"Well, let's see what sort of clue." Jack opened the case and frowned at the contents. "Syringes," he said. "And ampules filled with liquid."

"Trouble," said Abyssinia.

Jack nodded. "Of some kind, definitely. But what kind and for whom?" He snapped the case shut. "All right, I know a guy who should be able to run some tests on this stuff. We need to find out what it is."

"What about me?" Danny asked.

"You get to stay here for a few days, at least until you can move without bleeding to death." He stepped out the door. "I've arranged for some body guards. Go on in, ladies, he's all yours."

Two females, even more scantily clad than Abyssinia, crowded through the doorway and plopped themselves on either side of the bed, hemming him in.

"I am Lucy," said the dark-haired one. "Lucy Morales."

"I am Fifi Cachet," said the blond. "We are here to make you feel so much better."

Danny stared at the lace and satin and mounds of tempting flesh that surrounded him. He weighed the strength left in him, and found it hopelessly inadequate.

"Help," he moaned. "Help, help."

Danny's wound did not allow him to move around much and by the fifth day in bed, he was heartily bored, even with Lucy, Fifi, Abyssinia, and their friends checking in on him. He enjoyed their attentions, but he eventually caught on that their flirtatious manner was simply part of their job. They clearly appreciated that he was young and reasonably good-looking, but he was still a man. After watching them and listening to their talk, he realized that for these girls, men were simply a means to an end. They were catered to, cozened, and methodically lied to in order to extract as much money as possible.

"Why?" he asked Abyssinia after she returned from a session with a client. With Danny taking up her bed, she'd been using the room of another girl who was away visiting her mum in Eastside. The cosh and revolver thudded onto the bedside table and Abby drew a filmy wrap around her, collapsing into a chair with a sigh. "Why do you do this?"

She looked at him under her lashes and gave him a slow, seductive smile. "Because I love men so much, of course. I can't get enough of them. In return, I want to give them everything they want. To provide them with incredible pleasure and make them happy." She leaned closer, her ripe, luscious lips temptingly close to his own. "It's all I live for."

Beneath her sultry glance, he caught the expression of hard, bitter mockery. He reached up and touched her cheek. "No, Abby, why?"

Her eyes darkened and she slapped his hand away. "Don't you dare judge me, Danny Sundown! Who are you to question how I make my living? You took a bullet for a lousy paycheck that wouldn't even cover my lingerie expenses. We all sell ourselves, Detective. It's simply a question of how much we can get for the goods. What should I be doing? Working twelve hours a day, seven days a week at a factory that docks my pay if I step away to pee and fires me the minute I get hurt or sick?"

"I don't know," said Danny. "It's just that...all you girls...I never thought about what it might be like for you. Not until I got here and saw for myself."

"Most men don't know. They don't want to know, or care. It really is all about them and what they want. That's what they pay for, so that's what we give them." She jerked her chin at him. "Jack knows. He looks out for us. It's why we agreed to take you in."

"Is that the only reason?"

Abby's lip twitched. "He said you'd have some interesting vouchers to try and get your captain to approve. We do run a business here, Detective, and you're cutting into our profits."

He nodded. "I'll see you get paid. I'm beginning to understand how important that is." He held out his hand. "You have my word on that."

After a brief hesitation, she took it. "A pleasure doing business with you, sir."

"Likewise, ma'am." He held on for a moment. "You and the ladies here are worth every penny."

"Damn straight," she said, turning away, but not before he saw the glitter of tears in her eye.

"Am I interrupting anything?" Jack asked from the doorway.

"Just clarifying some business-related issues," Danny answered, pleased to see his partner. "Any news?"

"I'll leave you gentlemen to your work," Abby said, brushing past Jack in a manner that raised his eyebrows.

"What did you do to Abby?" he asked Danny. "She tried to distract me with that full-body frisk, but I saw her face."

Danny shrugged and then swore. He kept forgetting not to do that. "Just…gettin' a few things clear. I'm learning a lot, stuck here as I am."

"I'll bet you are."

"You know what I mean."

Jack nodded. "Yeah, I know what you mean." He sat down in the chair abandoned by Abby. "I, unfortunately, am learning very little."

"What about the stuff in the syringe case?"

"My guy says it's some sort of filtered blood product. Like a raw vaccine. He injected a small amount into a few test animals, which seem to be doing fine, if a little more cantankerous than usual. It's hard to tell with chickens. If it is a vaccine, it would have a protective effect only against the disease it was designed to fight. Unless we exposed the vaccinated animals to that particular illness, and none of them caught it, we'll never know what it's for."

An idea tickled the back of Danny's mind. "I don't know much about these here vaccines, but ain't they like weak versions of the full-blown disease?"

"Sometimes," Jack said. "But since this was taken from someone's blood, it's probably anti-body based, not disease-based."

"But what if the injections aren't meant to protect, but to infect?"

"I told you, the chickens are doing fine. No signs of illness."

Danny looked out the window, the moon was three-quarters full. "What if it don't show up right away?"

"Sundown, what are you thinking?"

"Lon," he said. "What if he wasn't bitten?"

Jack whistled. "A were-wolf shot? But no one's ever been able to indirectly infect someone with lycanthropy. You become a were-wolf by coming in close, personal, usually bloody contact with one - that's the only way." He paced around the room, thinking. "At least up until now. Walter Preminger was an alchemist - he specialized in making perfumes, stabilizing plant and animal extracts to keep them active. Maybe he found a way to keep the lycanthropy element active as well."

"He also wanted Rose."

"And Lon was in the way, so he infected him." Jack nodded. "It makes sense. But unless we wait for the next full moon, how can we know for sure? Those chickens aren't going to be sprouting fur, fangs, whatever, until then."

"Carlos might be able to tell. Take him with you."

Jack curled his lip. "You're asking me to take a coyote to sniff at some chickens? That's assuming I can even find the mangy mutt. He's made himself scarce since the spaghetti incident." Jack stood up. "I'll see what I can do, but I expect it'll have to wait until you're back on your feet. How's the shoulder?"

Danny fought back a grimace as he rotated it gingerly. "Much better. Another day or two and I'll be good as new."

Jack let out a skeptical snort. "Fortunately, I don't have to rely on your biased reporting. I'll check with Abyssinia on my way out." He glanced back. "Don't worry, partner, we'll get you out of here, probably sooner than is good for you."

Fifi squeezed past him carrying a bucket and a sponge. "Time for zee toilette a l'eponge, monsieur Daniel," she trilled.

"In the meantime," Jack said with an expression of great sympathy. "Try to bear it with the courage and fortitude that Granny Sundown would expect from one of her boys."

"I'll do my best."

"I just bet you will," said Jack with a bark of laughter and shut the door.

Midnight had passed, but it was only now, in the few hours left before dawn, that the Pierced Watermelon quieted down enough for Danny to sleep. It was not a restful slumber. He hadn't heard from Jack in two days, and he was worried. His body, not used to enforced inactivity, was restless and his mind spun. He never had trouble sleeping back on the ranch in Gravestone. Life there was simpler. If you could shoot fast and speak straight, most problems sorted themselves out quickly. Out on the frontier, where the land met the sky in a long unbroken line, a man could see what was between him and his destination. In the City, too many obstacles got in the way. How could you draw a bead on what was truly important? An image of Rose's face, eyes wide and trusting, swam into view. Danny's breath calmed and his heart slowed.

His peaceful slumber didn't last long. With the honed senses of a man who could tell when a rattlesnake had slithered into his bedroll, he knew there was someone else in the room. His hand crept to the bedside table, but all he grasped was a handful of taffeta.

"Looking for these?" Metal gleamed in the shadows. "I like your knife. It's sharp. Even the little curved bit at the tip. Good for skinning."

"Hyacinth," Danny breathed. "What the hell are you doing here?"

"Mum's working down the hall. I like to check on her, make sure she's okay. And see she doesn't run off after and blow all her pay on 'dust."

Danny felt anger stirring, knowing such stories were being told every day and hating how little he could do about it. "All right, but why are you in my room? Did the Omerta gang send you?"

"Nah, they still ain't paid me for knocking you out the first time. I'm here about Jack."

"Jack? What about him? Do you know where he is?"

"The Lady's got him. Her boys picked him up a couple days ago and took him to her. He ain't been seen since."

"The Lady?" he asked, but he knew who Hyacinth was talking about, even as he pulled himself up and reached for his trousers. First she'd taken Rose, and now Jack. Danny's shoulder throbbed with a dull ache, but he ignored it. It was past time to be up and doing. "Can you take me there?"

Hyacinth moved into a pale beam of light shining through the window. She was holding his weapons and a fresh shirt. "That's what I came for."

Danny was shaky getting down the stairs, but once outside, he felt better. There'd been something heavy and unsettling about the atmosphere in the Pierced Watermelon Hotel. Danny was thankful for finding such a refuge, though, and vowed to do right by the ladies who'd helped him. A grey shape bounded towards him, and he braced himself for Carlos' enthusiastic greeting. Instead, the coyote bumped against Hyacinth, who wrapped her arms around his throat.

"Scruffy!" she said. "You waited for me! Such a smart doggy!"

Danny raised his eyebrows at the coyote. "Scruffy?"

Carlos grinned sheepishly as Hyacinth scratched him under the chin. "What can I say?" Carlos growled. "I fed her and now she won't stop following me." Hyacinth's fingers found a sweet spot and his hind leg thumped as his eyes closed blissfully. "Can we keep her?"

Danny looked at the mismatched pair and sighed. "We'll talk about it later. Right now we've got to get Jack. He's in trouble."

"What kind of trouble?"

Danny remembered the ice-blue depths of eyes that could drown a man, even as he was drained bone dry. "The worst kind."

"Ah." Carlos nodded. "Girl-trouble."

"You got it, pardner. Hyacinth, which way to Lady Katherine's house?"

Hyacinth led them along a route that twisted down noisome alleys and through the broken shells of abandoned buildings. As bad as they looked from the outside, the derelict structures were even more nightmarish on the inside. It was here where the flotsam of Gristle Street flowed in on the tides of misfortune to collect in stagnant pools of misery.

Danny saw the pinched, smudged faces of children among the heaps of refuse and even with the evidence before his eyes, found it hard to accept that people lived like this. He watched how Hyacinth smoothly navigated the fetid maze, even as he would move across the familiar landscape of Nothingford Ranch, and knew that she must have grown up here. He wondered what the rest of her life would be like, with only this reference for the way things were supposed to be.

Slowly, the alleys grew wider and less filthy. Empty buildings were prudently boarded up. The graffiti, however, was more intricate than anything in the neighborhood of Jekyll's Gate. It occurred to him that it was simply safer to turn your back here.

"All right," said Hyacinth. "We're coming up on the rear garden. Be quiet and follow me."

It was full daylight, but the hulking mansion defied the thin sunlight, drawing about itself a chill cloak of brooding shadows. Danny thought of Rose, held hostage by that darkness and felt an urgency that even the news of Jack's disappearance hadn't instilled.

"You know a way to get inside?"

"Yeah," she said. "One of my mum's old boyfriends - Norman - showed me. He was a good bloke who didn't just knock her around and take her money. Norman had a delivery job that took him around to posh digs like this. The Lady saw him and he caught her fancy, so she kept him. He sneaked me into the kitchen most days for tea." She grew silent as she looked back at a memory that was both pleasant and painful. "He got so thin and pale, his eyes sunk back into his head. He started having trouble remembering me, even when I was talking right at him. All he thought about was getting back to Her. It was like he was burning with a fever that ate him away bit by bit." She tossed her tangled hair back, dismissing the loss as one of many. "That's how they go, vampire thralls, fading away until there's nothing left. Used up and tossed like empty bottles."

The heavily curtained windows revealed none of the house's secrets and Danny wondered if he would have to make a choice between rescuing Jack or Rose.

"Sorry buddy," he muttered. "I'm sure you'd do the same for me." He turned to Hyacinth. "Show me."

A glass pane in the basement service entrance slid aside, and the latch easily unlocked. She didn't make any fuss when he told her to stay outside. Her life was dangerous and unpredictable enough without invading a vampire's home. She faded back into the shrubbery, ready to run if any alarm was raised. Carlos, however, padded through the door, sniffing the dank air.

"This way," he said, heading for a set of rickety stairs, only visible while the door remained ajar. Once shut, the black was absolute.

Danny took a breath and paced the distance, arms stretched out in front, swimming through a darkness thick as Delia's coffee. His foot bumped the first riser and he ascended, wincing at every creak. Cobwebs brushed his face - remnants of the lesser vampires in residence. He bit back a cry as something more substantial swept against his hands, then realized it was Carlos' tail.

"Doorknob," the coyote said. "Coast is clear."

Danny opened the door and blinked as light hit his eyes. The hall was narrow and empty of all but dust. Carlos continued to lead the way. Much like the neighborhood, the house grew richer and more cared-for as they progressed.

"Wait," Carlos growled, and backed them both behind a strip of decorative molding. Danny caught a glimpse of an elderly man, dressed in rusty black crossing the hallway. They encountered no one else. The house was silent, as if the building itself were sleeping.

Carlos stopped before a pair of wide double-doors, heavily carved with voluptuous nymphs in less than decent states of dress. "Here," he said. "I smell blood," he added. "Nightfall's blood."

Danny's heart sank. "Go find Rose," he said. "I want her to be safe. Do whatever it takes."

"You sure? Anything happens to you, Delia won't be fit to live with."

"Rose gets hurt, *I* won't be fit to live with. Go."

Carlos gave a coyote shrug and turned away. "Trouble. Nothing but."

Danny took a deep breath, checked his gun, and opened one of the doors just wide enough to slip through. The room was dim, lit only by a dying fire. Among the opulent furnishings were a vast four-poster bed swathed in heavy brocade curtains and a chaise angled towards the fire.

Jack Nightfall sprawled on the chaise, wearing a loosely tied robe of black silk. He was deathly pale, dark punctures dotting the curve of his collar-bones. A small drop of blood had trickled down to nestle like a ruby in the hollow of his throat. Swallowing past the lump in his own throat, Danny reached out and touched Jack's shoulder.

Danny's wrist was grabbed in a vice-like grip as Jack's eyes snapped open.

"What the hell are you doing here?" Jack hissed in clear outrage.

"You...you...Lady Katherine brought you here."

"And what business is that of yours?"

"You didn't come out."

"So you thought you'd rescue me?" To Danny's shock, Jack pushed him away with a laugh. "Believe me, Sundown, the last thing I want is to be rescued."

Danny stepped back, frowning. "That's what Hyacinth says happens. They...the vampires make you forget everything else. Don't you see? She's controlling you."

Jack rose, shaking his head. "I appreciate the concern, but you've got it all wrong." He walked to the bed, gesturing for Danny to follow. He pulled back a curtain, revealing the recumbent form of Lady Katherine whose sheet-draped splendor surpassed the nymphs on her doors in every possible way. There was a faint flush on her cheeks and her red lips were curved in a smile of utter repletion. She was also securely tied to the bed by both her hands and feet.

The curtain fell back, but the image burned before Danny's eyes. Blood pounded through him like a railroad gang hammering spikes into a length of track.

"I'm the one in control, here, Sundown," said Jack. Danny stared at him, confusion, jealousy, fear, and desire warring in him.The door swung open and the old man in black stepped into the room.

The man was carrying a silver tray which he set on a table inlaid with semi-precious stones."I beg your pardon, Master Nightfall," he said. "I did not realize you were entertaining a guest. Shall I bring another glass of orange juice and more biscuits?"

"No, thank you, Carfax, that won't be necessary," Jack answered.

"Very good, sir. Will there be anything else?"

Jack glanced at Danny. "Is Miss Talma in her room?"

"Yes, sir. I took her some tea not an hour ago."

"Will you show Detective Sundown the way? He would like to speak with her."

"Of course, sir."

"But--" Danny protested.

"Jack?" A husky voice called from behind the curtains and both men's heads whipped around. "Won't you come back to bed, Jack? I need you."

"Go!" Jack hissed at Danny, grabbing the glass of orange juice and gulping down half of it. "I'll meet you back at the Watermelon…" He paused, as if gauging the limits of his own strength. "Tomorrow morning." He pushed Danny. "Talk to Rose. She knows something, but I don't think she knows it." The door shut and Danny found himself out in the hall with the nymphs and the butler.

"If you will follow me, sir," said Carfax.

The butler was ancient in appearance, but his insect-like limbs moved with deceptive speed and Danny was pressed to keep up. Several hallways and a winding stair passed in a blur until Carfax paused before a door of rich mahogany. Danny was pretty sure he glimpsed a brushy tail disappearing around a corner at the end of the hall.

"Miss Talma's room, sir," said the butler with the hint of a bow. He was gone, as swiftly as if he'd been folded up and put away with the linen.

Danny cleared his throat and knocked on the door.

"Who is it?"

The sound of Rose's voice did strange things to Danny. His response was an octave deeper than usual. "Detective Sundown, Miss Talma. May I come in?"

The door opened and she looked up at him, light blooming in her face as if seeing the sun rise for the very first time. All thoughts of the case vanished from Danny's mind. He'd spent a week surrounded by flirtatious, half-clad women. And the walls of the Pierced Watermelon, while decently thick, couldn't block out every noise. And just now seeing Lady Katherine - imagining what she and Jack had been doing, were almost certainly doing at this very moment...

He reached out, curled his hands around Rose's shoulders and pulled her against him, capturing her lips with his own. He drank deeply, as a desperate man finding a spring in a waterless wasteland. Her hands pushed against his chest, a murmur of protest fluttering in her throat. But he gentled her, wooing with his hands and his mouth, asking for her surrender in such a masterful manner that acquiescence was a foregone conclusion. She melted, her body molding itself against his as her arms wound around his neck, fingers weaving through his hair. He propelled them backwards until the bed hit the back of her thighs and they tumbled onto it in a tangle of limbs and inchoate desires that only grew more tightly entwined as the moments stretched into a timeless haze of heartbeats and breaths.When time slowed and reason returned, they eased apart. Rose touched his shoulder with an exclamation of dismay.

"You're hurt!" A small spot of red had blossomed against the white bandage, but Danny was far from feeling any pain.

He smiled and kissed her. "It's nothing, really."

"Was it...was it Lon?"

Danny frowned at her tone. He didn't want to believe she still harbored feelings for her ex and his arms tightened. She wriggled and he reluctantly let her go. She sat up and started fastening her clothes.

"He was there," Danny said, sighing as he pushed himself upright and did the same. "Shooting at someone else. I got caught in the crossfire."

She bit her lip. "How is he?"

"Angry. Dangerous." Danny answered shortly. He didn't want to talk about Lon. "Jack seems to think you might know something about Walter and the factory. Has Lady Katherine questioned you about it?"

"She did," Rose replied. "But it wasn't anything important. It was just something silly Walter wanted me to teach him."

"What?"

"An old nursery rhyme my Bibi sang to me."

"Beebee?"

"It means aunt, though really I think she was just an old friend of my mother's. She looked after me when I was a little girl. Once I had a terrible fright - a large dog had chased me and for days I refused to go outside. My Bibi taught me a little nonsense song, said it would make the dog completely harmless."

"Would you sing it for me?"

Rose did, an odd little tune with words that weren't in any language Danny had ever heard. From out in the hall there was a strange squeal and a thump. Danny was up by the door in a flash. He listened intently, but there was no other noise. He turned back to Rose who was sitting on the bed, her hair tumbled, her lips ripe with kissing. His heart twisted. He couldn't leave her here.

"Come with me," he said.

She shrank back. "Katherine said it wouldn't be safe for me to leave."

"I'll protect you, I promise."

Her eyes flicked to his wounded shoulder. "I...I can't. I know you'd try, but you couldn't, not all the time. I feel safe here."

"But Lady Katherine, she's a--"

"--I know," Rose said, staring at the floor. "But that makes her strong. Powerful." Their eyes met and he knew he'd lost. "I want to stay."

In two strides he was at her side. He pulled her up against him and kissed her with deliberate thoroughness. He leaned back and stared into her face, mollified by her dreamy expression. "All right," he said. "But I'll be back for you."

She glanced at him from beneath her lashes. "I hope so," she said with a smile.He didn't want to let her go, but Carfax would probably show up any minute with juice or digestive biscuits or something, so he kissed her once more to seal his promise and slipped out the door. Carlos was nowhere in sight.

"Carlos?" he whispered, heading for the corner where he'd seen the tail disappear. There was a slight scrabbling and a lean gray jack-rabbit hopped into view.

"Not a word," said the rabbit in Carlos' voice, only ludicrously high-pitched. "Not one damn word."

"But..." said Danny.

"Just pick me up and take me down the stairs. These spring-loaded hind-quarters would send me ass-over-teakettle."

"But...how...?" said Danny, tucking the jack-rabbit under his arm.

"I don't know!" squeaked the rabbit. "Some kind of magic. Get me outside where I can think. Through there." A large ear waggled, pointed.

Danny stepped into the kitchen. Hyacinth was sitting at a table, eating a sandwich. Danny's look was thunderous as he strode over to her.

"What?" she said. "The house was quiet and you were gone a long time. I got hungry." She stared at the rabbit in Danny's arms. Her eyes widened. "Scruffy?" she exclaimed, taking him from Danny and giving him a happy squeeze. "Oh, you are such a smart doggy! Look at you!" She grinned at Danny. "Do you think he can he change into anything else?"

Danny regarded 'Scruffy', who twitched his nose. "I reckon he can if he wants, but right now, It's time to leave."

"I thought you came here to get Jack."

Danny considered how much to say. "I spoke to him, and he says he's fine. I'm supposed to meet him back at the Pierced Watermelon in the morning."

The knowing eyes in the thin young face weren't fooled. She snorted. "The Lady's got him, doesn't she?"

"It seems…a mutual sort of getting. Dang it, he's a grown man! He'll do what he pleases. Let's go."

Once outside they headed back the way they'd come, Danny in no fit mood to talk. He was almost glad when a dark figure detached from the shadows.

"Your partner is a fool," Lon growled. Danny wondered how Lon knew about Jack's new girlfriend when a soggy white bundle landed at his feet. It was a dead chicken. "They got the serum back. Do you know what that means? Do you?" Lon moved closer, his hands clenching and unclenching as if yearning for something to throttle.

The anger that rose in Danny wanted to let him try. "Maybe I would if you'd bother to tell me. What'n hell's going on? Is it a were-wolf serum or not?"

"Yes," said Lon pushing his snarling face towards Danny. "And no." His nostrils flared and a mad flame leapt in his eyes. "You've been with her. Rose. You've *been* with her!"

The tension between the two men snapped and they lunged at each other. Danny's wiry strength, bolstered by his fury allowed him to block the first two blows, but it was an uneven contest. The next fist doubled him over, only to be straightened up by an undercut to the jaw. His legs slid out from under him as a blur of silver flashed across Lon's ribs, leaving a trail of red.

"Leave him alone!" Hyacinth hissed in her deep mugger's voice, brandishing Danny's wickedly curved bowie knife. Vaguely Danny wondered when she'd taken it off him. Lon roared and lashed out with his fist. Just before it connected, he saw that his attacker was a child and managed to open his hand to grab her wrist instead.

"I don't hit kids!" he yelled, shaking her. Undaunted, she hauled off and hit him in the nose with her free hand. He roared and took hold of that hand as well. She connected with a well-aimed kick and he grunted. He pinned her arms against her sides, picked her up and dropped her into a wheelie bin.

A gruff voice coughed. "I suggest you step away from my friends."

Danny smiled. He knew what was coming. He only wished his vision wasn't so blurry. He spit out a gob of blood and tried to sit up for a better view of the show.

Lon turned, taking in the lean, gray-haired, very naked man standing before him. "Who the hell are you?" he asked.

"Someone you don't want to mess with," the old man said, seeming to levitate off the ground as he spun around, his leg lifting in a graceful arc that had his foot connecting with the side of Lon's head at the peak of his rotation.

Lon bent over, grunting, but straightened quickly and launched himself forward. A flying side-kick landed in the center of his chest, slamming him against a brick wall. He managed to lift his arms and block the roundhouse kick, but the old man spun like an auger, the heel of his other foot connecting with Lon's jaw. Then the real dance began and Danny looked on happily until Lon, recognizing the better part of valor, retreated from the whirlwind and fled.

The old man watched him go, then looked at Danny, eyeing his blooming bruises. "Idiot," he said, holding out his hand and pulling Danny up.

"You do so well with two feet," Danny told him. "Why're you always running around on all fours?"

Carlos smiled. "You would understand if you walked a mile in my paws."

"I'll pass, thanks," Danny said.

"Hey," a voice called from the depths of the wheelie bin. "I could use a hand here."

Danny gestured at Carlos' lack of clothing. "Can you change back into a coyote?"

Carlos squinted thoughtfully, but his nose immediately started twitching. "No," he said grimacing. "I'd just end up as a rabbit again. I need to go back to the tribal lands, perform a cleansing ritual and sweat out whatever magic caused my transformation." He shrugged. "Don't matter. It's nearly time for my human phase anyways."

"Fine, but what do we do about you right now?"

"Can I borrow your jacket?"

Danny made a face, but handed it over and Carlos tied it around his waist. Then they hauled Hyacinth out of the bin. She backed away from Carlos, brandishing the knife. After a few steps she stopped, tilted her head and frowned. "Scruffy?" she asked.

"Yep," he answered.

"Oh, okay," she replied. "We should get you some clothes, then."

"You two head on back to the Watermelon," Danny said.

"What about you?" Carlos asked.

Danny looked out into the night, feeling the ache in his jaw and a deep restlessness. "I need to find a drink."

Carlos looked as though he would like to say something, but he closed his mouth, shook his head and put a hand on Hyacinth's shoulder. "C'mon, girl, best let the man get on with his evening. But first you need to give back his knife."

The knife had vanished somewhere among Hyacinth's mismatched bits of apparel. "Do I gotta?" she asked. "I heard of a job that pays good money for knife-work." They both looked at her and she rolled her eyes. "Not *that* kind of job. This is legit. On the level. Honest."

Danny remembered how she'd defended him, fearlessly taking on a brute like Lon. He thought about what her life was like here, preying and being preyed upon. Any edge he could give her was little enough. "Sure," he said. "Keep it until I can get you your very own."

"You mean that?" she asked, her voice filled with the memory of too many broken promises.

"Yes," he said deliberately. "And if for some reason I can't, Carl…Scruffy here will see to it. Right, Scruffy?"

"I will," said Carlos in the manner of a man taking a sacred oath. As Danny knew he was.

"Okay," she said. Her hand crept into Carlos' and Danny watched the pair walk away. He flashed back to his own childhood, the feel of Carlos' leathery hand wrapped around his as he learned what the old coyote had to teach. He wasn't sure if he could remember any of it, in this place, on this day, and shook away the thought.

"A drink," he said. "That'll help." Though he knew how many times he'd said it, and how seldom it actually worked out that way, but it was the only answer he had.

Beneath the throbbing of his bruises, Danny felt a familiar urge. If he'd been on a horse, he'd have dug in his spurs and ridden hell-bent for the horizon. But there was no horizon here. Just a lot of people fighting for not enough space.

"Too long, too long," he muttered. He'd been cooped up among walls far too long and he felt the need to move and breathe freely. In Gravestone you could point yourself in a direction and keep going straight without meeting a single soul. This place was a maze of twisting streets and dead-end alleys, all seething with life - or what passed for it here.

There was a maze of canyons a few days' ride from the Nothingford Ranch where men pursued by the law would run, thinking to escape. But whenever Danny and Sheriff Noon pulled up in front of the narrow entrance, they'd simply set up camp and wait. Within a week, a lone straggler might stagger out of the canyon, wild-eyed and babbling about voices and visions, pleading to be taken in. Most who went in never emerged.

The crooked streets and deep shadows of Gristle Street reminded Danny of that canyon and he felt that he might start babbling any time. Holding himself in check, he walked until he found a shop that carried a familiar brand of Gravestone whiskey. The feel of the bottle in his hand was like a promise of home.

"Is there an open place around here?" he asked the clerk. "A park or a green space without any buildings?"

"Well, there's Wolvercote Acres," the clerk answered. "The 7a stagecoach goes that way. Should be by any time. But you don't want to go there. It'll be dark soon."

"Yes, I do," Danny said, paying for his whiskey. "Thanks."

The clerk shrugged. "It's your funeral," he said.

Danny flagged down the stage and pulled himself up beside the driver. He noted the sleek horses and well-oiled harness.

"Nice rig," he said.

"Yep," the driver replied. "I've learned it pays to be ready for trouble. Always managed to outrun it when it shows up. Never had a horse go down, never had a piece of tack fail. I been driving this route ten years without losing one customer - leastaways not so long as they kept their arms and head inside the carriage." He tapped his whip against a sign on the vehicle that reiterated the warning.

Danny's hands itched to feel leather against his palms again. "I've done my share of driving," he said. "Mind if I take a turn?"

"That depends," said the driver.

"On what?"

"On what you've got in that bag."

Danny pulled out the bottle far enough to show the label. "Old Snake Bite," he said.

The driver grinned and passed over the reins as Danny gave him the bottle. He cracked the top and took a mouthful. "Ahh," he breathed. "That'll wake the dead, it will." He leaned back, happy enough to give Danny the occasional instruction between sips.

Danny's tension eased. There was comfort in the sight and smell of horses - the feel of their mouths running up the reins. For all the power he'd felt driving Rose's automobile, he missed this kind of connection. He controlled the horses, but unlike a car, they could choose to obey or not, often making better decisions than the driver. These two knew their route, so he had very little to do, and settled in to enjoy the ride.

He felt the change in them as the road sloped upwards. They grew tense, picking up speed at the same time he felt a breeze that hadn't spent its life sneaking through alleys and bending around corners. A bird flitted past, heading for a tree outlined against the sky. He sensed the cool emptiness of quiet spaces as the wrought-iron arch inscribed with 'Wolvercote Acres' rose up on the left.

"This is where I get off," he said, pulling the reluctant horses to a stop.

"What?" spluttered the driver, shoving the bottle back at Danny and grabbing the reins. "Are you crazy? Night's coming on!"

Danny swung down as the driver whipped the horses and sped off, driving like the newly awakened dead were on his tail. As he passed beneath the iron archway, his boot heels sank deep into a mossy cushion and silence wrapped itself around him like an old quilt. The deeply angled sunlight cast an amber glow, submerging the world in a bottle of whiskey. Dozens of narrow shadows reached elongated fingers towards Danny. Crosses, pillars, straight and curved oblongs, squat buildings, graceful shapes with wings, others twisted in grief - he was surrounded by monuments of stone dedicated to the dead.

"Boneyard," he said, taking a rueful drink. "Figures."

He roamed among the stones as the light dimmed, reading inscriptions that were still visible on the weatherworn stones. When darkness arrived in earnest, the silence changed, became aware. He felt the touch of invisible fingers, the whispers of disembodied voices. The dead resented his warmth, his substance, his breath - all the things they no longer had.

But one didn't grow up in a place called Gravestone, in the company of a totem spirit like Carlos, without learning something about ghosts. Danny respected the dead, but he wasn't afraid of them. Selecting a raised box tomb to sit on, he poured a cap full of whisky and placed it where he estimated the owner's head would be. Then he sat and waited. The plucking and hissing whispers ceased, though the air still felt heavy and Danny could sense the crowd that clustered around his chosen tomb.

He raised his bottle in a toast. "To you, the unquiet dead," he said, drinking. "If you have something to say, I'm listening."

They came, with their pain, their anger, their despair and laid it at his feet. He nodded in sympathy, knowing how much it must hurt to be torn from life too soon, leaving behind unfinished business and unresolved wrongs - forever deprived of the power to make them right. But Danny offered up his own need to see justice done. He'd dedicated his life to it, and the ghosts responded to that. Night deepened, stars wheeled, the level in the whisky bottle lowered. Then, like a brace of candles being snuffed out by a sudden gust of wind, the ghosts were gone. He felt the hair on the back of his neck stir.

"How charming," came a voice rich and low, the sound of which he'd not been able to get out of his mind. "Spirits with the spirits." Lady Katherine Delonghi glided into view, as ethereal and luminous as any ghost, the pale fur of her lynx coat glimmering in the light of the nearly full moon. "So tell me, Detective Sundown," she said, settling beside him as though the stone slab was a parlor sofa. "Do you come here often?"

Danny wasn't afraid of the dead, but the undead were another matter altogether, especially this one. For lack of any better idea, he handed her the bottle.

"First time," he said. "You?"

Katherine laughed and tipped her head back, pressing the bottle to her lips. He watched her neck undulate as she drank, wondering what it would be like to grow fangs and press them against that pale skin, sliding them into her cool flesh. When she gave the bottle back, he tried to relieve the dryness of his mouth with a long whiskey wash, but it didn't help much.

"Do I come here often? I know my way around the place," she said in answer to his question. "The Delonghi crypt is a few hundred meters further in."

"Do you keep a key hanging on a nail inside, just in case?" He knew he was being rude, but she disconcerted him like no woman ever had.

"Electronic palm-reader, actually," she answered. "One of the perks of owning a part interest in Wolvercote Limited."

He couldn't tell if she were serious or not. The stunning loveliness of her features confounded his ability to read her expression. "Where's Jack?" he asked bluntly.

"Where I left him, I presume. In my bed." She leaned closer. "But didn't you mean to ask how he is?"

"All right then," he agreed. "How is he?"

"Alive," she said. Her lips curved. "Quite sound of mind and free of will, if thoroughly exhausted in body, I assure you."

He was afraid to meet her eyes, not because of what he'd heard about a vampire's gaze, but because of what she might see in his. "Then tell me why," he asked, "you are trying to de-rail our investigation by distracting my partner?"

She shook her head. "You underestimate Jack Nightfall, Detective. He is quite…extraordinary." Her smile was surprising in its softness. "My interest in him has nothing to do with your case. I am still a woman, as well as a vampire. And despite popular opinion, we do not simply feed on mortals and toss them aside. We have not lost our capacity to feel love and experience deep and lasting desire. On the contrary, we have time to explore and appreciate the pleasures of the flesh, in all their wondrous variations." There was a lambent glow in her eyes, as if she gazed upon a recent memory. "*All* of them," she murmured huskily.

Danny took another drink, wondering how he could feel so warm while sitting on cold stone with his jacket wrapped around a naked ex-coyote. "Wonderful," he said. "I'm happy for you both, but that doesn't explain what you're doing here. I don't reckon us meeting like this was an accident."

"No, I had you followed from the house," she said with blunt candor. "Whatever has happened between Jack and I, I do admit to having an interest in your case."

Danny snorted. He realized he'd had much too much to drink, but he couldn't do anything about it now. "Of course you're 'interested', Countess. Walter, Lon, Rose - they all worked at your damn factory. The whole thing stinks, and not of perfume."

She held up a finger. "Yes, they were all employees of my company, and I am concerned that the situation could end up reflecting badly on more than just my business. You see, Detective, I am being considered for a seat on the Narrative City Council to represent Gristle Street. It is a great opportunity, both for me, and for the denizens of this district. Until now, Gristle Street has been considered too unstable and fractured to be granted a full voting presence on the Council. But I have been working very hard to convince those in power otherwise. This...unpleasantness could jeopardize all my progress."

"So you want it to go away? Get swept under the rug?"

"No!" she snarled. "I want it solved! I want you and your incredibly sexy partner to prove that law and order can work in Gristle Street. And not only to justify the confidence of the Council, but for the residents of Gristle Street. To show them that they don't have to fight all their own battles, or resign themselves to a life without any hope of help or protection."

He stared at her, the fog of his mind trying to make sense of what he was hearing. "Why?" he asked. "Why do you care? You can say what you like about people as if we were pretty butterflies in a jar, but you're no phil...pilant...do-gooder."

Her eyes narrowed and her smile was not soft. "Indeed, Detective. Perhaps Jack is well-matched after all. You are right, I am not a 'do-gooder'. I want influence and control far beyond what I hold now. Those petrified fossils on the Council have been sitting undisturbed while Gristle Street languishes in the dark ages. It's time to disturb them, and to do that, I need to occupy a seat at the table. Since the Jekyll's Gate riots I have been working to reconcile the various Gristle Street factions - and it's working. The vampires, the weres and the humans are learning to coexist in a grudging semblance of peace. Whatever Walter was involved in could destroy that precarious balance."

"The weres," Danny muttered. "He found a way to create them without direct infection." An image of Carlos transforming from a coyote to a rabbit bounced through his mind to the tune of a strange little song. Ideas that had been floating and bumping upon the tide of whiskey suddenly clicked together. "Rose, her Bibi's song, it can transform one animal into another. With that, he could make any kind of were he wanted."

"Oh, very good, Detective Sundown. Now all you need to figure out is why."

"But Walter is dead."

"Indubitably," she said. "But he must have told someone what he was working on, or they found out. His equipment was taken, his notes and the serum."

He tried to focus on her face, but it was nothing more than a pale blur, like a second oval moon against the darkness. "That wasn't you?"

"No, it was not me. Like you, I chose to pursue Rose instead. That choice may cost us both dearly." She shrugged. "But when the house is burning, what do you save? The Picasso or the pussycat?"

"Pussy," he murmured, finding himself sinking backwards, the star-filled sky spinning overhead. Something soft drifted over him."Sweet dreams, Daniel," a voice whispered and he thought he felt a kiss as smooth and cool as satin brush across his lips. Perhaps the ghosts had returned to haunt him some more, but he was too tired to care. He pulled the blanket under his chin, wondering why the mattress was so hard. The stars swirled and spun into darkness, like water down a drain.

When a beam of determined sunlight slipped past a stone and landed on his face, Danny felt as though he was being stabbed between the eyes with a flaming pencil. He sat up with a curse. An empty whiskey bottle rolled off the grave and landed unbroken on the mossy ground. A white-gold coat of lynx fur slipped down over it. Danny stared at it with a strange mixture of horrified curiosity. He clapped a hand to his neck and his heart tumbled when he found no trace of puncture marks. He was sure it was the sour film coating his mouth that made his relief taste strangely like disappointment.

He took the empty bottle with him when he left, but one stone angel now looked less cold and forlorn with the lush coat wrapped around her slender gray shoulders.

Jack was at the Pierced Watermelon, sitting in the room where the ladies took breakfast. He looked like hell. From the expression on Jack's face when Danny walked in, he knew he didn't look any better.

"Coffee?" Jack asked.

"Yeah," Danny answered. They worked their way through most of a pot before speaking again.

"Captain wants us to come down and report, now that you're back on your feet."

"Any idea what he'll say about Lon still being loose?"

"Only one way to find out," Jack replied, lurching upright. He gripped the edge of the table until he steadied. He grinned at Danny. "Haven't felt this knackered since the bachelor party we threw a mate down on Lover's Lane. There were these succubi strippers..." he paused, lost in a warm haze of nostalgic reflection before shaking himself loose. "We had to call in medics to resuscitate him. The ambulance siren was the only reason we got to the church on time."

Danny stood up and closed his eyes against the pain. "No sirens today, please."

"I feel for you, buddy," said Jack, clapping a hand against Danny's still-tender shoulder. "But the captain isn't known for expressing his opinion at less than full volume, so brace yourself."

Jack was correct, and Danny fought to rein in his temper as the captain lit into them about their unkempt appearance, the lack of updates, and especially their failure to bring in Lon. Danny noticed how he kept scratching his forearm in the place Lon had bitten him and wondered how much time they had before the next full moon. Katherine had gleamed in the bright silver light of the nighttime graveyard, so there wasn't much time at all, a few days at most. What would happen to the captain then? What about Walter's serum and whoever had stolen it back? Did they plan on using it? What if they already had? A feeling of urgency filled him, but there was no way the captain would allow him to get a word in. The tirade eventually wound down, but Danny was chained to his desk for the rest of the day filling out overdue paperwork. Jack was sent off on a series of minor local calls. They exchanged glances whenever Jack returned, but the look on his face forbade any discussion. The captain was still deciding their fate, and until he gave the word, they were in procedural limbo. At the end of his shift, Danny had no choice but to go home to the small, dingy apartment left empty since he started on this case.

It wasn't empty now. Carlos sat cross-legged on a blanket in the middle of the floor. He was wearing some of Danny's clothes and there was a smell of burning in the air.

"What is that?" Danny asked, wrinkling his nose.

"Cleansing sage," Carlos replied. "The vibrations in this place are dismal, and you'd not taken out the garbage. I emptied the ice box, too. One of the take-away curries escaped before I could catch it, though. I think it's holed up in the bathroom."

"Well, thanks for that," Danny said, slumping onto the narrow bed. "How is Hyacinth?"

The coyote's face creased in a smile. "I like her, she has a warrior's spirit. She introduced me to Lily, her mother. Such a sweet, beautiful lady, with a soul too fragile for the world she finds herself in. We got on quite well."

"So what are you doing back here burning leaves and liberating expired curries?"

"Lily and Hyacinth went off to look into some jobs being offered down by the docks."

Danny remembered Hyacinth saying as much. "Well, I hope it works out for them." He fell back onto the mattress and draped an arm across his face. "If I don't make any progress in this case soon, I may be looking for a job, too."

As he spoke of the captain's fury and his own frustrations, exhaustion crept over him and he barely heard Carlos' reply.

"Two days," the coyote said. "When two days have passed, the moon will be full and I will be fully a man. All the changing ones will become their other selves, the wild spirit within bursting forth to be free to hunt, to kill. That is the Way, and it is a good way. But it is different here; there is too much pain, too much danger. I will seek guidance." His low, melodic chanting, as familiar as a lullaby, led Danny into a deep, dreamless sleep.

In the morning, the apartment was silent and empty, except for the curry snoring behind the commode. It burbled angrily at Danny as he washed and shaved. He left the window cracked, hoping it would get the hint. There were flourishing colonies of feral curries for it to join who would teach it to survive on the streets.

The day went no better than the one before. The captain was, if possible, in an even fouler mood, and Danny didn't see Jack at all. The only bright spot was the absence of the curry when he got home, though his pillow smelled suspiciously of old boots steeped in cumin.

Half-way through the next day, Jack stopped at his desk. There was a peculiar expression on his face.

"Looks like someone left a package for you outside," he said.

With a cautious glance towards the captain's office, Danny headed for the door, Jack following closely. At the bottom of the steps a man lay bound in many loops of heavy rope. It was Lon, alive but definitely not kicking. Danny recognized the style of the knots, he often used them himself when dealing with obstreperous livestock.

"Carlos," he breathed.

"Tell that old coyote I owe him a steak," grinned Jack. "This should get the captain off our backs and us back on the case."

"Assuming he believes there is a case. He's had time to read my report on Walter's serum, but so far, nothing."

"Well, let's get this guy inside and behind some solid iron bars. Then we'll take on the captain."

The first few people they passed merely stared at what they carried, but soon everyone was standing and clapping, accompanied by whistles and cheers. Lon had not made many friends during his last visit to the station.

"What'n hell's all the racket about!" bellowed the captain, charging out of his office.

"Just escorting Mr. Daninsky to his cell," Jack answered. "It appears he was civically minded enough to turn himself in."

"Danin…" Captain Foley approached and took a good look at their captive, his eyes narrowing dangerously. "Turned himself in, did he? After knocking himself out and tying himself up?"

"He was afraid he might have second thoughts about doing the right thing?" Jack suggested.

The captain growled. "Just lock him up and get back to work."

"Back to work?" asked Danny. "Do you mean--"

"Yes! Back to Gristle Street on whatever wild were-goose chase you got caught up in." He ground his teeth together. "I received a call from Countess Delonghi, wondering where her 'favorite policemen' had gone. Apparently knowing you're on the beat makes her 'feel safe'." He rolled his eyes. "Whatever. She's got powerful friends on the Council, so if she wants a couple of tame police dogs at her beck and call, I got no problem handing your leashes over."

Jack and Danny's eyes met and quickly dropped.

"Thanks, captain," answered Jack.

"Don't thank me." The captain's expression was bleak. "You cross Lady Katherine and you won't have a chance to remember what a teddy bear I was." He turned to leave. "Oh, and Sundown, she also asked if you would be sure to return Miss Talma before dark. She doesn't want her granddaughter out late. Apparently," he said, his voice heavy with suppressed feeling, "there's a full moon tonight."

"But I haven't seen Rose since… ." A shock ran through Danny. "Are you saying Rose…Miss Talma is missing?"

"Lady Delonghi seemed to think she was with you." The captain loomed. "Is there some reason why she might think that? Have you, perhaps, forgotten that Miss Talma is a material witness to a crime which you are investigating?" Captain Foley stepped back. "Not that I care about the private lives of my officers - what you do on your own time, with whom, is your business." Jack and Danny's eyes met again and dropped even more quickly. "But make sure it *stays* your business, not mine! I suggest," he said with deceptive mildness, "that you talk to Countess Delonghi, assure her that you are indeed on the job, and find out if Miss Talma might require some assistance."

He stomped away, the door to his office closing behind him with a slam that rattled all the windows in the building.

"Take me with you." The voice from inside the cell was rough with pain.

"What?" said Danny to Lon. "We just locked you up. There's no way we're letting you out again."

"They've got her," said Lon. "They lured her out and they've got her. I can help you find her."

"How? You can't possibly track…" he trailed off.

"That's right," Lon laughed, though it sounded like a painful cough. "In a few hours, I'll have a nose better than a bloodhound's, and I know Rose's smell. Ohhh, I know it. I could even trace her steps in the perfume factory days after she'd been there."

"Dammit, no! I'm not letting you loose so you can terrorize Rose again!"

"Danny," Jack said, "they took Rose. That means they know about the song, and they're planning to use it. Whatever is happening is likely going down tonight. Rose may be our only lead. If we find her, we'll find the guys who took Walter's serum, and stop them from using it."

"And Rose…?"

"Will they need her again, once they learn her little trick?"

"I don't…I don't think so."

"Then I think we'd better find her. And unless you have any idea where she might be, Chuckles here is our only chance to find her before she becomes just another loose end to be snipped off."

Danny's fist closed around an iron bar, his knuckles going white with his desire to deny the truth, but it couldn't be done. "All right, Jack. Cut him loose."

They hustled Lon out the back without incident - no one expected Detectives Nightfall and Sundown to kidnap their own prisoner. Jack also 'borrowed' a squad car. Danny calculated the charges hell was racking up for them to pay, but Rose's soft, trusting eyes stared at him and he knew she was all that mattered. No price was too high to keep her alive and safe.

Lon was quiet, hunched in the backseat, wearing two sets of handcuffs on his wrists.

"I didn't think anything could bring you down, Lon. What'd he hit you with?" Jack asked over his shoulder.

"Which time?" Lon said with a grimace. "I don't know who that guy is, but I know what his foot tastes like." He paused as if sifting through competing flavors. "It didn't taste altogether human."

"He's a shape-shifter," Danny explained, somewhat reluctantly. He didn't want to have a friendly conversation with this man. "He prefers paws and fur most of the time. Been that way since I've known him. And long before I was around, if the stories he tells are true."

"He can...he can live like this? With a...an animal running wild in his head?"

The pain in Lon's voice ran deeper than any visible bruises and Danny couldn't help but recall that he'd been infected totally unawares - maliciously targeted by Walter Preminger. To test his serum, or drive him away from Rose - most likely both - it was not a fate that Lon had in any way deserved. Sympathy edged past Danny's guard, despite his overwhelming desire to dislike the man.

"Carlos isn't your average were." Words of comfort did not come readily. "But I've known others like you who've made peace with themselves. It's not easy, but it can be done."

Lon shifted. "They're safe? Around other people?"

Jack snorted. "Buddy, I don't think anyone in this car is particularly safe to be around. But it's our job to take responsibility for the consequences of our actions, no matter what drives them. Besides, without the danger, where's the fun?" He took a corner with a squeal of wheels. "In my experience, safe is boring." The car screeched to a halt. "We're here." They were parked across the street from Lady Katherine's mansion. "You stay with our friend while I talk to Countess Delonghi." Jack told Danny.

"Just talk?" Danny asked.

Jack's mouth quirked. "Yeah, just talk. Business before pleasure." He opened the door. "We're too close to the answers to screw it up now. Don't worry, I know when keep it buttoned. The Lady understands, too."

Remembering her words in the graveyard, Danny believed she did. "Okay. Make it quick."

Jack glanced at Lon. "Right."

The silence after Jack left was oppressive. But Lon knew things that were important to the case - possibly to finding Rose.

"You killed Walter," Danny said.

"Yes." The voice was sullen, but defiant. "I'd do it again, too. He didn't change shape like me, but he was a monster. He did terrible things."

"What things? Other than injecting you with his serum, what else was he involved in?"

"I don't know. It happened at the warehouse, but I can't remember anything else. It was a full moon." The eyes that met Danny's in the rear-view mirror were haunted. "It was...awful. I got away, but I knew I had to stop Walter. He deserved to die."

"But this didn't end with his death. Someone has taken Rose - one of the gang from Omerta's?"

"I don't know. I thought I broke them up, but whatever Walter's scheme was, it's still going on. They stole the serum back, they got to Rose. Whatever happened at that warehouse, it's going to happen again."

Danny remembered Carlos' reaction to the warehouse. He was one tough old coyote who'd seen more than anyone's fair share of horror and misery, but that place had shaken him deeply.

"Bad medicine," Danny murmured. And now they had Rose. He knew Lon was thinking the same thing, but it wasn't something they could talk about - not and maintain the fragile cease-fire that existed between them. The heavy silence descended once again.

Someone rapped on Danny's window. His gun was out before he had time to think, but on the other side of the glass, Carlos grinned and waved. Danny searched for the window knob and rolled it down.

"What'n hell are you doing here?"

"Wondering why you're driving around with the guy I went to so much trouble to deliver to you." He opened the rear door and sat down next to Lon. "Hello," he said, nodding amicably. He turned back to Danny. "I thought you wanted to keep your job?"

"A slight shift in priorities," Danny explained. He'd caught sight of Jack coming out the front door. In the half-shadowed entryway, Katherine held him back for a less-than-business-like parting embrace.

Carlos whistled appreciatively. "Well now," he murmured. "It's a strong man who can walk away from an invitation like that."

Danny agreed, but Jack only managed one step before turning around and giving back as good as he'd gotten, maybe even a little extra. Then with a firm wrench to settle his disarranged clothing, he marched with grim determination to the car. It was only when Jack got the door open that Danny saw his knees give way. With a sigh, he collapsed into the driver's seat. He glanced into the rearview mirror.

"Hey Carlos," he said.

"Hi Jack." Carlos smiled.

"What did you find out about Rose?" Danny asked, impatient for action. The hours of daylight were trickling away.

"Earlier today, Miss Talma received a message, delivered by a 'dirty-faced urchin' last seen in our company."

"Hyacinth?"

"That would be my guess. Miss Talma left soon after."

"She just let her go?"

"That's what I asked. We were apparently under the misapprehension that Miss Talma was being held against her will. Countess Delonghi assured me that this was not the case. Miss Talma was always free to come and go as she pleased."

Danny glared at Jack. "All right, but you aren't going to tell me that Lady Katherine didn't have her followed."

"Now how would you know that?" Jack smiled and started the car. "They were able to trail her as far as the docks, then they lost her."

"The docks again." Danny stared out the window as the buildings whipped by at a steadily increasing speed. "That's where this is going to go down."

"Yep," agreed Jack. "We just need to be there when it does." He sent the car fish-tailing around a corner and recovered with the smoothness of much practice. He pressed the gas until the engine screamed. "You might want to buckle up, it's gonna be a bumpy ride.

To Danny, it felt like a race with the sun. Shadows were lengthening and he heard Lon stirring restlessly in the back seat. Carlos wouldn't be much help when Lon changed. He always complained that he was at his weakest during a full moon - soft, feeble, *human*, whereas Lon in wolf form would be nearly unstoppable.

"Danny," Jack said softly. "Take these." He took one hand off the wheel and reached into a pocket. Danny felt the smooth metal cylinders pour into his palm. Bullets - bright, shiny ones.

"Silver," Jack said. "I took them off that security guard at the perfume factory. You might need them."

"Thanks," said Danny, trying not to think of the problems those bullets could solve. It wasn't Lon's fault he was about to turn into a were-wolf - but he was still dangerous. "And," said that small voice Danny never wanted to believe was his own, "he wouldn't stand between you and Rose anymore." He slammed the door on the voice and locked it. Still, he reloaded his gun with the silver.

The unmistakeable smell of the river grew stronger. A thick yellow fog gathered, clinging to the car as if looking for a way in. Jack turned parallel to the river and slowed, squinting at the derelict warehouses and rotting piers silhouetted against the smoldering sky.

"What are we looking for?" asked Carlos.

"Any sign of unusual activity."

"This is Gristle Street, most activity could be described that way."

"Just keep you eyes peeled," Jack growled. The car crept along in silence.

"There, by the water," said Carlos, not waiting for the car to stop rolling before opening the door and hopping onto the pavement. Jack and Danny both got out, though Danny stayed close to the car, uncomfortable with leaving Lon unattended. Carlos didn't try to be stealthy, openly approaching a group of ladies standing on one of the ramshackle docks. They were in the process of boarding a wide, barge-like craft, carrying mops and buckets with them. One stepped forward, greeting Carlos with a smile. Her face was sweet, but puffy and careworn. They chatted briefly, his grizzled head bent over her silver-blond one. He helped her onto the boat and it puttered off. He returned, wiping a smear of pink lipstick from his cheek with a sheepish smile.

"Hyacinth's mom, Lily," he explained before anyone could ask. "Said she hadn't seen or heard of anything unusual along the river this evening."

"I'd be more use if I could get out and walk," Lon growled. "The wolf is getting close, I can feel it, I can feel everything."

Carlos nodded. "He's right. I can't smell anything but this damnable fog anymore. It's like I'm wrapped in cotton wool." He shuddered. "I don't now how you stand being so blind all the time."

Danny looked at Jack, who shrugged. "It's your call. You three could go on foot, following Lon's nose, while I can cover more ground with the car. Is your phone charged?"

It was. The captain had loomed over Danny the previous day until he plugged it in. He and Carlos took Lon out of the car and Jack drove away, sluggish vortices of yellow fog coiling in his wake.

Lon flexed his shoulders, the chains of his handcuffs rattling. He inhaled deeply and Danny could see the seams on his shirt straining. He kept his hand near his gun, but Lon merely jerked his head towards the river.

"This way," he said and moved off at an easy lope.

The setting sun blazed across the oily surface of the river until Danny expected to feel waves of heat coming off it, rather than the clammy chill of the oncoming night. Coming on too quickly. He picked up the pace in response to his growing sense of urgency, but Lon inched away, bent close to the ground, sweeping his head from side to side, searching for one delicate scent among hundreds of rank odors. In a final searing burst, the sun slipped into the river, not even a ripple to mark its passing. Darkness closed in and the world held its breath, waiting. On the other side of the sky, the moon thrust itself upwards, bloated and swollen with its stolen light.

Lon stopped, hunching over with a grunt of pain. Danny loosened his gun in its holster as Lon snapped upwards, throwing his head back in a scream that modulated into a full-throated howl. Bathed in silver light, he changed, his face reshaping itself, fur sprouting wildly. Wrenching his arms apart, the chains on both sets of handcuffs snapped like they were made of twine. He clawed at his shirt, ripping it to shreds. His hands hit the ground and he shuddered, the transformation rippling along the rest of his body. The handcuffs slipped from his reshaped forelimbs. With a leaping twist, he escaped from the rest of his clothing and a black-furred wolf stood glaring at Danny and Carlos, lips lifting from its gleaming fangs.

Danny aimed his gun at the space between the flaming eyes, cocking back the hammer. He knew how fast the wolf could move and how little warning it would give. His finger tightened on the trigger.

A low hum rose from his left and Carlos lifted his hands slowly, swaying as he voiced a calming chant. The wolf's gaze flickered between the two men. The fur between his shoulders smoothed and the teeth disappeared. Danny eased the hammer down, raising the gun slightly.

"Rose," he told Lon. "We need to find Rose."

The ears pricked and the wolf spun, sprinting away.

"Damn!" Danny swore and took off after, Carlos beside him. The wolf flickered in and out of the shadows, flying over obstacles that no one, man or wolf, should be able to leap. Danny tried, scraping his hands and forearms raw against a towering wall of brick, but it was no use, Lon was gone."This is stupid," Danny panted. "We might as well be running in circles. We need a lead."

"Wait, I hear something," said Carlos as if on cue. He turned towards the river.

Danny listened. The ragged puttering carried clearly across the water. "It's just that barge again." He took a closer look, no cleaning ladies this time, instead the boat carried a group of large, grizzled men, several with beards and fur hats that left only a small strip of weathered skin visible between them. "Who're those men aboard? They don't look like they're from around here."

"Hunters, trappers, I'd say, probably from Eastside," offered Carlos. "Yes, I recognize Sven Boar-sticker. He once skinned a deer in under ten minutes."

"Is that fast?"

"It is when the deer is still running."

"Who's the short guy with them?"

The men on deck shifted, giving them a clearer view of the slight figure. "That's no guy," said Carlos.

"Hyacinth!" Danny exclaimed. "She delivered the note that lured Rose out of Lady Katherine's house. She probably knows who wrote it!" He lifted his hand and shouted. Hyacinth saw who it was and waved back, smiling. She held up Danny's Bowie knife, light glittering on the long blade until the fog closed in, swallowing the knife, the boat, and everyone on it. "Dammit," he said. "We've got to catch up with them."

"There's a boat here," Carlos observed, peering over the edge of the dock. "But it's chained to the post."

Danny eyed the warped, rusted skiff with skepticism, but the motor looked operational. "Right," he said. "I commandeer this here vessel for official NCPD business." He tested the chain. There was no way to break it with the tools he had on hand. "Stand back," he told Carlos. He kicked at the mooring post until the rotten wood of the dock gave way. He pulled the chain off and tossed it in the boat. "No use hitchin' your horse to a bad rail," he said, grinning. "I had an ill-tempered mare who taught me that one. Now get aboard and let's hope the water is thick enough to hold us up."

If the outboard motor had run on curses, they would have been speeding down the river like a bullet. As it was, getting the persnickety thing started and keeping it going was barely within the scope of Danny's non-existent mechanical knowledge. But after much pulling and swearing, the motor stuttered into life and they were in soggy pursuit of the barge. It would be impossible to catch it up, but Danny had hopes that it would soon pull over to let off its passengers. He looked down at the scummy water lapping at his boots, rising slowly as the river discovered innumerable leaks along the hull joints. It had better be soon. This water was not like the old swimming hole back home. Nameless, bloated objects rolled to the surface as they passed, some bumping spongily against the hull and releasing gaseous exhalations that forced Danny to hold his breath.

No, swimming the River Stynx was not an option. This had better be a quick trip.

But where in Gristle Street would a boatload of Eastside huntsmen be going? At night? Under a full moon? And why was Hyacinth with them? They had been looking for unusual activity, and to Danny's mind, this fit the bill. Find the barge and they'd find their link to Walter's serum...and Rose. He took out his phone and texted Jack. Even if they didn't make it, Jack Nightfall could have a chance.

The waterfront scrolled past, dark, silent, empty. Nothing moved except the fog, bunching in thick clouds, braiding into murky ribbons.

"Danny, look," said Carlos. Ahead on the right, a beam of light escaped through a crack in a blacked-out window. The bulk of the moored barge slouched in the shadows of a ramshackle warehouse. Before Danny could adjust the tiller, the engine coughed, sputtered, and died with a sound Danny recognized as a final death rattle. The river spun the skiff carelessly downstream, away from the dock.

Ahead, a skeletal structure thrust dark fingers through the fog - the Hyde Bridge. Floating under those age and fire-darkened beams, exposed to whatever lurked beneath them, was not something Danny cared to do. He crouched in the boat and yanked out the narrow wooden thwart he'd been sitting on. Carlos followed suit and they paddled fiercely for shore. It was working, but they were still being carried past the warehouse. Danny dropped his paddle and grabbed the coiled chain. Whirling the loop over his head like a heavy lariat, he tossed it with a grunt around the last possible mooring post. Hand over hand he hauled them forward until they could jump onto the dock.

Releasing a stream of oily bubbles, the skiff filled with water and sank, pulling the chain taut as it vanished into the murky depths.

"Good timing," Carlos remarked.

"Yep," said Danny, already turning his attention to the warehouse. "Looks like Lily and the other cleaning ladies ended up here as well." He pointed to a careless tangle of mops and buckets stashed behind a pile of oiled timbers.

"Now why would they just dump them there?" said Carlos. "It makes no sense." Grim lines pulled his face downwards. "I have a very bad feeling about this."

"Right with ya, pardner," Danny said, creeping towards the broken window. "Let's see what we're up against."

He remembered the empty cages and the hooks from the other abandoned warehouse. But tonight everything was in use. Limp, pale-furred animals were being taken from the cages by the huntsmen and hung onto the hooks by ropes tied around their hind legs. There'd been about a half-dozen huntsmen on the boat, and all the ones in view held wicked-looking skinning knives. He didn't know where the boat driver was and there was no sign of Rose. He wondered if Jack was anywhere nearby. A little back-up would be nice when tackling such a large target.

A sharp intake of breath came from Carlos. The older man's face was ashen in the light of the window. "Oh Great Spirit, no!" he choked, leaping for the nearest door, shouting. Danny had no choice but to follow. They burst into the warehouse, every bearded face and skinning knife turning towards them. Carlos didn't seem to care. "Hyacinth!" he called to the girl. "Stop! Your mother's one of them!"

Then Danny understood. The animals were unusually large, pale-gold foxes. All the women on the first barge had been blond, including Hyacinth's mother, Lily. "Oh gods," he said, feeling sick.

"I don't know who you gents think you are," one of the huntsmen growled, stepping forward with his knife pointed in Danny's direction. "But we're doing a job here. So I suggest you walk away and leave us to do it."

A swift series of metallic clicks was followed by the huntsman's sudden and violent exhalation as a telescoping baton jabbed into his midsection. "NCPD," said Jack Nightfall, stepping into the light with his badge raised. "Detectives Sundown and Nightfall of Central Division. I suggest you drop your knife unless a broken wrist is on your wish list." He looked around. "That goes for the rest of you, too."

"Sven," said Carlos to a vast, blond man with a beard like a haystack. "They're women. They've been shape-shifted into foxes."

"Carlos?" said the man. "Be it thou, ye olde poultry-thiefe?" He looked at the fox dangling from his hook, his brows screwed together. "Women, ye say?" He took the animal down, gently cradling it in his arms, stroking the luxurious fur. "She be breathing, and has taken no hurt I can see, but I ken not what ails her." He looked at the other men. "Ye heard what he said, take them downe, with proper care, minde."

"I don't think so," said a cold voice. Two men emerged from a doorway at the far end of the warehouse. They both carried large, heavy handguns. "The boss wants this evening's business to proceed as planned. The detectives will come outside with me. My associate will make sure everyone finishes what they started. The old man will provide additional incentive." Without blinking, he shot Carlos in the stomach. "He bleeds until you're done." Then he made a peculiar sound, like a fish gulping for air. His head dropped and he stared in disbelief at the hilt of Danny's bowie knife protruding from the center of his chest. His knees buckled and he crashed to the ground. The other man swung his gun towards Hyacinth, her arm still extended from throwing the knife. A shot rang out and a small dot appeared in the center of the gunman's forehead. A red trickle ran between his eyes as he toppled backwards. Danny looked over at Hyacinth before lowering his gun, and she nodded. Then they both ran towards Carlos.

"I'm all right, I'm all right," he said querulously, slapping their hands away. "It was only a silver bullet. They don't do much damage, even during a full moon."

"Silver!" said Danny. "But I thought were-wolves--"

Carlos glared at him "How many times do I have to tell you, I'm not a were-wolf! Silver is sacred to my people. Do you think a totem spirit would be vulnerable to a sacred metal?"

"So what are you vulnerable to?"

"What kind of a dang fool would I be to tell anyone that? Even you?" He straightened up with a grunt. "Don't you have somewhere else to be? What about that girl of yours?"

"Rose," Danny recalled with a shock, and moved quickly towards the far end of the warehouse. Jack went with him.

"Stop right there," said a voice from the doorway. It sounded familiar, but Danny couldn't quite place it. Then Rose appeared, the expression of abject terror on her face driving all capacity for thought from his mind. His gun snapped upwards. "Oh, I wouldn't if I were you," said the man with his arms locked around Rose and his thumb on the plunger of a hypodermic stuck into her neck. "Unless you want to give this lady a fur coat that you'd have to cut off her."

The sick fear of true helplessness grabbed Danny by the throat and squeezed.

"I remember you," said Jack. "You're the security guard from the perfume factory."

The guard sneered. "I'm much more than that now. Walter Preminger left me the key to a fortune, and nothing is going to stop me from walking out of here and starting up again someplace else."

"You're insane," said Jack. "Changing people into animals and then killing them just for the fur, it can't possibly be worth it."

"He be righte, ladde," offered Sven. "These be nice pelts, I grant ye, butte the furrier market be righte poorly at present. 'Tis why we be here, lookinge for work." The other men nodded, murmuring assent.

"Idiots!" the guard spat back. "You have no idea what certain people will pay for a genuine were-skin coat. And now that I know this pretty girl's song, I can make them to order." The guard groped Rose in a way that made Danny's eyesight blur behind a haze of red heat. It took all his strength not to throw himself at the man and rip the smirk off his face. "So if you two defectives will step aside, I'll be going. Too bad about tonight, but there'll be another full moon next month, and there are plenty of people in the world that nobody will miss."

Having no choice, Jack and Danny let him drag Rose to the door. They couldn't stop him without risking her. He gave one bark of laughter as he stepped onto the dock, framed in moonlight. It changed into a hoarse cry of terror as a vast black shadow fell from the roof and landed on top of him.

"Lon!" cried Danny as he lunged through the door. The guard lay screaming on the ground, the hulk of the were-wolf straddling him until with one juicy crunch, he fell silent. Ignoring the dangerous proximity of the beast, Danny dropped to his knees beside Rose who was huddled on the ground. "Rose!" he whispered as he scooped her carefully into his arms. "Are you hurt?"

She opened her eyes, they were wide and staring. Her mouth moved but nothing came out. One hand uncurled and Danny saw the hypodermic. The plunger was pressed and the vial was empty. "Rose," he breathed. "No." He pressed his face against hers, willing her to be fine, denying the truth of his failure to protect her.

Silver light poured over them as the moon sailed across the sky. She stiffened in his grasp, her bones shifting, becoming loose and fluid beneath her skin. A whimper of pain built in her throat until it emerged as an agonized howl. Danny kept holding her, his own breath coming in painful gasps as he bargained with all the gods he knew to let him take this from her. She thrashed wildly, breaking his grip, rolling onto her hands and knees. He reached out to her once more, but found himself pulled away.

"No, Danny, there's nothing you can do. Let it go," said Jack, locking an arm across Danny's chest as he fought to return to Rose. But it wasn't Rose any more. Thick, mahogany-colored fur covered the slender lupine creature, as she thrashed free of her clothing and stood panting on four trembling limbs. The black wolf watched, his eyes glowing as he licked the guard's blood from his chops. Danny pulled out his gun, aiming at Lon, but again, Jack interfered. "No," he said. "The rules are different here. He did what needed to be done."

"And that's what I'm doing," said Danny, his voice shaking.

"I'm sorry about your girl, but this won't help."

The black wolf turned his gaze on Danny, an unmistakably human understanding flickering within the yellow fire, and Danny knew he couldn't do it. He let his arm fall to his side. "Dammit," he said. "This isn't how it's supposed to end."

Lon trotted toward Rose, who growled, and he lowered his head, regarding her with a hopeful expression. She sniffed cautiously, showing her teeth when he moved too close. He danced around her, grinning as she snapped at him. He bounced on his forelegs, wagging his tail until she relented, the bend of her neck inviting him closer. Soon they were chasing one another. In a few moments they leaped into the shadows and disappeared into the night.

"C'mon, partner," said Jack, putting his hand on Danny's shoulder. "Let's go back inside and do our job."

"Is that all there is?" asked Danny shoving his gun back in its holster. "The job?"

Jack gave the moon a tight, mirthless smile. "Not always, no," he said. "But sometimes it's the only thing that keeps us going."

Calling into the station Jack asked for assistance. The bodies would need to be identified and statements taken from the huntsmen. Jack also requested information on the dead security guard, specifically an address.

"We need to make sure Walter Preminger's notes and serum are taken care of this time." Jack said. "That knowledge is just too damn dangerous."

Danny didn't say anything. His hands curled into fists and he stared at the moon's reflection, stretched and deformed by the swirling surface of the river.

Hours later the scene was cleared and Danny and Jack headed back to the station. Carlos stayed behind with Hyacinth to care for the drugged foxes who'd been returned to the cages for safe-keeping. Two officers were instructed to keep watch and to speak with the ladies once they changed back.

"Where's the captain?" Jack asked the officer at the desk. The sergeant jerked his chin in the direction of the lock-up without saying anything. In Lon's old cell, a burly wolf paced, pausing now and then to gnaw irritably on a large stew bone someone had tossed in. He showed his teeth to the two men, growling in a familiar manner.

Jack assessed the situation. "Guess our report can wait until later."

"Detective Nightfall?" a junior officer trotted in, holding a clipboard. He glanced uneasily at the captain and stood well back from the bars. "We had a report on the address you requested. Apparently there was a fire earlier in the evening. It's being investigated as suspicious, but there's not a lot left. The flat was completely destroyed."

A light clicked on in Danny's mind which had been dark and clouded since Rose's transformation. The guard wouldn't have set fire to his own flat. But who else might have done it? And would they have known enough to take Walter's research using the fire to obscure the theft? What were the chances of this happening all over again?

A slender thread of cool air brought the scent of musk, ambergris, and the sharp tang of iron. Danny knew at once who it was.

"Detectives Sundown and Nightfall," Lady Katherine purred, entering the space like a cat making itself at home. She glanced at the cell. "Captain Foley," she acknowledged with a polite head tilt. "Congratulations on solving your case. And may I add my personal appreciation for your hard work on behalf of all the residents of Gristle Street?" She fastened her eyes on Danny. "I understand my granddaughter has experienced some...alterations in her situation, but, as I have cause to know, not all such changes are unwelcome. She can take care of herself now, with a strong mate to protect her as well."

Danny winced. The woman knew which buttons to push to inflict pain as well as pleasure. She'd led all of them around since the beginning, knowing a great deal more than she would ever admit. He'd bet that she'd had a hand in the fire as well, not that there'd be any proof. Could they ever aspire to being knights, rather than pawns in this woman's twisted games? And what part had Rose been made to play?

Anger burned in him, hot and dangerous. "Your fur coat," he said. "You're not wearing it tonight."

She showed him her teeth then, knowing he was dangling his suspicions of her in front of Jack. The masks were off and she dared him to make Jack choose between them.

He couldn't do it. He couldn't be sure he'd win. His eyes dropped, ceding her the pitch.

"The coat, yes," she continued smoothly. "It was given to me as a gift. But it's not a very appropriate statement, politically speaking. I am, after all, a newly elected member of the Narrative City Council, and as such, I must consider the sensitivities of my constituents." Her gaze slanted at the captain again.

"The Council voted you in?" said Jack. "May I offer my own congratulations, then."

She moved to Jack's side and smoothly slid her arm through his. "Yes, you may, Detective. I'm actually having a small celebration at my home tonight. I was hoping you would be willing to be there as a representative of the close relationship I intend to establish between the law and myself. In an official capacity, of course."

"Of course," Jack agreed. He broke his eyes away from hers long enough to glance at Danny. "Sundown, will you--"

Danny waved him off. "Yes, yes. Go on."

He watched the two walk away. The captain snarled, gripping the bars between his jaws, trying to find a way to express his frustration."Yeah," Danny muttered. "I know how you feel."

Danny didn't stay long after Jack had left. He tried filling out some preliminary reports, but couldn't focus. Some time before dawn he gave up and went home. There was a soggy rustling in the alley and he put out a bowl of yoghurt for the curry before collapsing onto the bed, emotionally and physically exhausted. It was easier being shot, he decided as he was sucked down into a morass of ill-formed thoughts and uneasy dreams featuring skinning knives and girls transforming into golden-eyed wolves.

He blinked himself awake when the burning gold became the unwelcome glare of sunlight. Carlos was sitting on the floor a few feet away.

"You are up," Carlos said.

"Don't know if I'd go that far," Danny grunted. "What time is it?"

"Mid-afternoon. I've been waiting some time."

"Waiting," he said as he stretched, feeling every ache of the last several weeks. "For what?" The events of the night before slammed into him. Rose. His failure to protect her was too raw, and he turned away from the memory. He tried to remember that there were others they had managed to help. "Hyacinth," he said. "How is her mother?"

Carlos nodded. "Lily and the other ladies are all right. After the barge dropped them off, they were given 'vaccinations' and sent into the cages to clean them, but the soap contained wolfsbane. Since they'd been infected with Walter's lycanthropy serum, it rendered them unconscious just before they changed. That way they could be skinned without killing them first. A dead were-wolf - or fox - returns to its human form. No fur, no profit."

Danny shuddered. "Lon was right about Walter being a monster. And that guard…he got better than he deserved. He must have read Walter's notes to find out about Rose and her song - a transformation spell, really - that she learned as a child. If only I'd figured it out sooner, maybe I could've--"

"--Danny, don't." Carlos shook his head. "Rose is alive and she's with Lon - who did everything because he loved her. They'll be okay."

Carlos might be right, but Danny drew little comfort from it. His tone was sour as he replied to Carlos. "Well, thanks for the update." He pushed himself up off the bed. "Now if you'll excuse me, I'd like to take a shower."

Carlos rose. "Danny, I've come to say good-bye. I'm returning to Gravestone."

"Oh, of course, you need to set your own magic straight," said Danny. He was surprised at how empty he felt at the thought of Carlos leaving. It was like a last tie to his home was being cut. But he was a grown man now. He didn't need anyone nurse-maiding him, no matter what Delia thought. "Well, good-bye, then." He held out his hand.

Carlos looked at it, then pulled the younger man into a hard embrace, thumping him soundly on the back.

"Idiot," he said gruffly, pushing him away. "I also wanted to tell you that Lily and Hyacinth are coming with me. I'm going to take care of them."

That revelation staggered Danny. "But you...you're...you've never..."

Carlos scrubbed a hand through his grizzled mane. "I know, I'm a confirmed old bachelor. But maybe it's finally time for a change. Hyacinth deserves better than this life. I can give it to her - and to her mother."

"But Lily...Jack said she's a Moondust addict. That's not something you get over."

A grin curled Carlos' mouth. "Not any more. One thing about being a were - most drugs burn right out of the blood. We can't *get* high." He barked. "Maybe because we're already there. Don't worry about Lily, Danny, Hyacinth and I will look after her. Oh, I nearly forgot." He bent down and pulled Danny's bowie knife out of his boot. "Hyacinth wanted to make sure you got this back. She doesn't want to play with knives anymore."

"I guess I can see that," Danny replied.

"She wants to learn to shoot a gun instead."

Danny put his hand over his eyes and groaned. "Gravestone will never be the same." He felt a hand grip his shoulder.

"Nothing ever is, boy. We just got to learn to move with it."

Danny nodded. "You taught me a lot about that." They walked towards the door.

"I think maybe some of it actually sunk in," said Carlos. "You've not done too badly, here."

"Is that what you'll be telling Delia?"

Carlos snorted. "Something like that, with the rougher edges trimmed off."

"I'd appreciate it. Otherwise she might get it in her head to come down and see for herself."

"You could always head her off and come home for a spell. Make sure things don't change too much in your absence."

"I will," said Danny. "Tell Delia I'll be coming home, one of these days."

"Just don't leave it too long," said the old coyote, and he was gone.

Danny stood in his empty flat, listening to the silence. He thought about going in to work, but decided there was something else he needed to do first and went to get cleaned up. In the alley, something banged an empty bowl impatiently against the wall.

The door of the Pierced Watermelon Hotel was answered by a scowling urchin. She was new, the dirt on her face only recently rearranged.

"We ain't open yet," the urchin said, swinging the door shut.

Danny jammed it with his foot. "Tell Miss Abyssinia that Detective Sundown is here to see her on a matter of business."

The urchin eyed him with deep suspicion, but let him in. "You wait here."

Obedient to such a fierce command, Danny leaned against the polished wooden counter, taking in the atmosphere that had grown so familiar during his weeks of recuperation. Perfume and tobacco scent floated over a deep earthiness, drowsy now in the late afternoon, soon to wake into a sharper, more bitter-sweet draught with the coming of night. He could hear her descending the stairs - the soft rustle of diaphanous fabric and the rhythmic creaking of a straining corset. He turned and caught his breath. She was indeed a stunning woman.

"Well," she purred. "Detective Sundown, as I live and breathe. What brings you back to us so soon?"

His voice plunged deep. "I've come to pay my debt, ma'am."

"Really? I am impressed." She sauntered closer.

"It seemed important." He pulled out a bag. "Hold out your hands."

She regarded him with a lifted eyebrow, but cupped her hands together. He poured the contents of the bag into them until they overflowed with bright silver cylinders, dozens upon dozens of them. The warehouse guards had kept all their guns loaded with silver bullets, knowing what they truly needed to fear.

Abyssinia gazed at the glittering ammunition with a smile of unfeigned delight. "Oh Danny," she whispered. The bullets pattered onto the carpet as she pulled him in for a kiss. "There's more than enough to cover what you owe." Danny felt as much as heard her words against his lips, and the promise behind them.

He stepped back and looked into her eyes. "Put it towards my tab, would you?" he said, running a finger along her jaw before turning to leave.

"Detective!" she called out as he pulled the door open. "You're not planning to get shot again, are you?"

"I can't make any promises, Miss Abby," he said. "But the next time I visit, I'd prefer it to be under my own steam."

"You see that it is, Daniel Sundown. I want to be sure you get your full money's worth."

"Ma'am," he smiled, touching his hat. The sun was burning its way below the rooftops as he descended the steps. The opening bars of 'Home on the Range' buzzed softly from his pocket, and he pulled out his phone. He pushed what he thought was the right button and held it near his face. "Hello?"

"A body's been found in the River Stynx, just past Jekyll's Gate," said Jack Nightfall.

"Is that unusual?" Danny asked, remembering the anonymous shapes he'd encountered in the river, rolling and bobbing in oily slicks of bubbling gas.

"No," said Jack. "But this one was wearing a tuxedo with the ID of a Little Tokyo Council member in the pocket." Danny was glad he hadn't been within earshot of the Captain when that call came in. "Do you want me to pick you up?" Shrieking brakes and angry horns could be heard over the full-throttled roar of Jack's car.

"That's okay," said Danny, his stride lengthening as his legs took him unerringly towards the broken-tooth roofline of the Cauldron. "I'm on my way."

Printed in Great Britain
by Amazon